BLOOD MONEY

Seth Klugg, manager of the Springfield Cattlemen's Bank, is out of town, seeing the proposed new railroad as an opportunity for drumming up business. Meanwhile, the three strangers who ride into Springfield see in his absence an opportunity of their own ... Kidnapping the assistant bank manager and his wife, they proceed to hold them hostage, awaiting the return of Klugg — the only man who knows the combination for the bank's safe. But Klugg has made many enemies, and is riding alone across open terrain — what will happen if he fails to return?

D. D. LANG

BLOOD MONEY

Complete and Unabridged

LINFORD
Leicester

First published in Great Britain in 2013 by
Robert Hale Limited
London

First Linford Edition
published 2015
by arrangement with
Robert Hale Limited
London

A catalogue record for this book is available
from the British Library.

ISBN 978–1–4448–2466–7

Published by
F. A. Thorpe (Publishing)
Anstey, Leicestershire

Set by Words & Graphics Ltd.
Anstey, Leicestershire
Printed and bound in Great Britain by
T. J. International Ltd., Padstow, Cornwall

This book is printed on acid-free paper

To my wonderful family:
Ben and Cheryl, Leah, Scott,
Ellie Rae and James
and of course, Sue

1

The explosion, when it came, was far greater than had been expected. But then the bank robbers hadn't known what to expect.

They'd never used dynamite before. More to the point, they'd never attempted a bank robbery before.

★ ★ ★

The manager of the Springfield Cattlemen's Bank was out of town, trying to drum up new business from the outlying cattle ranches that surrounded the town in the hundreds and thousands of acres of prime grass land.

This was cattle country and the prospect of a proposed railroad had sent Seth Klugg, the manager, on a mission with silver dollars shining in his eyes.

He could see great things for Springfield; more importantly, he could see great things for Seth Klugg.

It was his chance to finally get control of this backwater town and get some real money and power. He had, through the head office in Chicago, received privileged information concerning a certain railroad project, and Klugg intended to take full advantage.

Klugg was an ambitious and ruthless man. He had few, if any, friends in Springfield. He treated the citizens of the town with contempt in the main: he saw them as below his station.

He'd been sent to Springfield almost five years ago — a temporary assignment, he'd been told.

In truth, he was despised at head office: a good banker, reliable, an astute mind and able to manipulate deals in the bank's favour. But as a human being, Seth Klugg left a lot to be desired.

The prospect of the railroad coming was the opportunity Klugg had been waiting for. The town had prospered as the cattlemen moved in.

Homesteaders suddenly found that their mortgages and loans were being called in with very little notice and their land was being auctioned off by the bank.

By Seth Klugg.

He'd formed a company and no one knew that he, along with a silent partner, was the sole owner. He was able to snap up the land at ridiculously low prices.

Initially the town had suffered. Fresh produce was in short supply and prices rocketed as everything, except beef, had to be shipped in.

The cattlemen began, with Klugg's help, to run the town. The money rolled in from the ranch hands and drovers, as thousands of cattle were bred and driven to the markets to the east and north. But very few of the townsfolk prospered. The one exception was the saloon, the Golden Horn.

It was owned by a one-time card-sharp called Wilbur Enright, who'd acquired the saloon in a rigged poker game that ended in bloodshed.

The then-owner, Al Beamish, who prided himself on his poker skills, accused Enright of dealing from the bottom of the deck. Enright had drawn and fired in the blink of an eye.

Enright 'allowed' Beamish to win the first five hands easily; the whiskey flowed and Beamish, already $300 to the good, thought Lady Luck was on his side, exactly as Enright had planned.

Beamish became careless in thinking he was unbeatable and that the lanky stranger had picked the wrong time and place and man this night.

His carelessness cost him his life.

The Golden Horn had a new owner.

Witnesses confirmed that Beamish had drawn first, but whiskey has a way of affecting a man's judgement and capability.

The sheriff had no alternative but to do nothing.

The saloon prospered and an alliance, hardly a friendship, was forged with Klugg, as Enright became his biggest customer in town and more and more cattlemen were employed on the ranches and needed to spend their money.

In the West, news of a town prospering spread quickly, attracting the dregs of humanity out to make a fast buck anyway they could.

A town council was formed in an attempt to stem the lawlessness of the once-peaceful township. The sheriff, Clint West, was given three deputies and the jailhouse was extended, allowing for another four cells to accommodate the drunks and vagrants who nightly chanced their arm.

The three men who rode into town early one morning, Wes Brown, Dale Smith and Clay Leghorn, seemed peaceful enough.

They checked into the only boarding-house in town. Found the livery and paid for their mounts to be fed, watered and bedded for two nights. Then they visited the barber shop, got their beards trimmed and their hair cut and took a soak in the tub to wash away the trail dust, before venturing into the Golden Horn.

All in their early twenties, they presented no apparent threat, their baby-faces making them seem harmless as they checked out the saloon.

But their sinister intentions belied their outward appearance.

They had only one reason to be in Springfield.

The bank.

They ordered beers and found a table at the back of the saloon, from where they could see every corner of the large, smoke-filled room. A safe place to sit, with no one behind them.

This was to be their first foray into crime. They'd tried honest work, but the money they earned was a pittance — the straight and narrow, they reasoned, was for the mugs.

'Howdy boys!' A wizened and obviously worse for wear old-timer bumped into their table. 'Spare a dime? I sure could use me a drink right now.'

'Seems to me you've had plenty already, old-timer,' Wes answered. He flipped a coin in the air, but caught it before the old-timer could get his hands on it.

Licking his lips, he fixed his gaze on the silver dollar held in Wes's palm; he waited.

'Sit down a whiles,' Wes offered. 'We'll get you a beer. Busy little town you got here.'

'Sure is,' the man drooled. 'More money than ever coming in, banks fit to bursting,' he added, still licking his lips in anticipation.

'That a fact?' Wes replied. 'Get the man a beer, Dale.'

'On my way,' Dale answered.

'So,' Wes continued. 'This bank, big is it?'

'Naw, tinpot building but it sure got itself a fancy safe from back East.'

'That a fact?' Wes mused.

'Sure thing, mister, fancy-looking thing it is, too, set in the manager's office. I see'd it many times as Mr Klugg, he's the manager, likes to keep his office door open. 'Cept when he's screwin' some poor homesteader out of his land!'

Wes grinned. 'Seems like he ain't much liked here in town then,' he said.

'Man's hated. Got no friends in this town, an' thass a fact.'

'He live local?' Wes asked, just as Dale returned with beer.

'Got hisself a fine house right off Main. Picket fence and fancy-looking too. But he ain't here at the moment; left ol' Luther Parry in charge while he goes about seeing the ranchers. By all accounts, he be drummin' up more business, or trying to.'

'This Luther Parry, he live local too?' Wes asked.

'Sure 'nough. Him an' his wife got a small place just down the street aways. Nice little house it is too. Mrs Parry got

8

some fine drapes covering them winders. Purty lady too.' The old-timer grinned lasciviously.

Wes smiled, looked towards Dale and Clay and then tossed the dollar coin to the old man.

Busy finishing his beer, and thinking of many more to come, the old-timer missed the coin and it rolled on to the sawdust covered floor.

'Obliged, mister, I thank ya mightily,' he said as he slid to his hands and knees to get hold of the dollar coin.

★   ★   ★

It didn't take Wilbur Enright long to suss out the three strangers. He wasn't for one minute fooled by their appearance; there was something about them that rang warning bells in his brain.

He kept a wary eye on the three men; having already fended off four attempts to rob the saloon of its nightly takings, Enright trusted no man. He checked his .45, satisfied himself that it was loaded and tucked his long coat behind the holster for easy access to the weapon — should the need arise!

The evening passed relatively peacefully: the usual rowdiness, the occasional disagreement, a few drunks who shouted their mouths off, only to be ejected unceremoniously onto the boardwalk, kicking and screaming and wanting to take on anyone who came near.

But no gunplay. Indeed, a quiet night.

Still, Enright kept a wary eye open.

The three men relaxed, ordered another beer each and enjoyed a smoke. As far as they were aware, they had attracted no attention as they watched the occupants of the saloon. The bar girls were doing their usual flirting for overpriced and watered-down drinks; the rannies were trying to attract their attention, hoping maybe to get laid at some point; drunks staggered from one table to another looking for any glass unattended that might contain beer or whiskey, unaware that some of the glasses held other less intoxicating substances. Some had been pissed in by the watching cowboys and they howled as a drunk downed the liquid, before realizing too late what it was.

Eventually the long trail ride caught up with the three young men and, after downing their beers, they stood and left the saloon, heading back to the rooming-house and sleep.

Enright watched them leave and breathed a sigh of relief. For some reason he decided they were trouble.

Their casual amble as they crossed the saloon didn't fool Enright; he noticed that, despite their tidy and clean appearance, their boyish faces and affable expressions, their holsters were low-slung, their weapons, all Colt .45s, immaculate; one of the men had twin holsters and the butts of his pearl-handled six-guns nestled in ornately tooled leather. They sure weren't for show.

Reaching the rooming-house, they

found the front door locked, so Wes took to hammering on the door. It took only a few moments for the frail Ma Dooley to unlock the door.

'Sorry, gents, but I always lock the door come nine. 'Specially when the place is empty. Come on in.'

'Thank you kindly, ma'am,' Wes said. The three men removed their Stetsons and entered the house.

'Coffee in the pot and there's some pie if'n you fancy some,' Ma Dooley said.

'Again, thank you ma'am, but we're dog-tired so I think bed is where we're headed. Goodnight, ma'am.'

'Breakfast is at eight,' Ma Dooley told them, then added, 'Sleep well gents.'

The three men entered their room and Dale lit the oil lamp. It was a large, square-shaped room with four single cots, a dresser, wash-bowl and stand and a small threadbare rug. No palace, but the cots were comfortable after four nights sleeping under the stars.

They clambered into their beds. Before turning out the light, Wes, who was unelected leader of the group, said, 'I'll wake you when we're ready to go. OK?'

'Sure thing, Wes. We'll be ready.'

In a matter of minutes the only sound in the room was a gentle snoring as the three men slept.

* * *

It was Wes who woke first, as promised. He checked the hunter in the near pitch-black room, lit only by the eerie blue glow from a full moon. It showed 4 a.m. Perfect, he thought.

He eased his frame out of the bed and made his way carefully to the window. Their room looked out on to Main Street and he cautiously pulled back the thin cotton drape to take a look-see outside.

As he expected, it was deserted, not a light showed anywhere. Springfield slept.

Rousing Dale and Clay, he put a finger to his lips.

'Deserted outside, boys, time to make our move.'

Dale and Clay stretched, yawned and got out of bed.

'Hot damn!' Clay whispered. 'I sure had me a fine sleep.'

'Me too,' Dale added.

'What's the plan, Wes?' Clay asked.

'Simple. We get this Luther Parry outa his bed and make him open up for us, then we take the cash and ride on out. Clay, you git to the livery and saddle up the horses. Don't forget the saddle-bags, we might need that dynamite. Then lead them down to the bank. Me an' Dale'll take the rope, then we'll head down Main Street, find the Parrys' place and git our man. OK?'

Silently, the three men left the rooming-house. Clay headed for the livery, while Wes and Dale made their way down Main Street, heading for the home of Luther Parry and his wife.

2

Main Street was bathed in the bluish light from the moon, slightly brighter than it had at first appeared to Wes through the window of their room.

But deserted it certainly was. Not a sound split the silence as they made their way looking for 'fancy drapes'.

As they neared the end of Main, Wes suddenly stopped and raised his right hand.

'What?' Dale whispered.

'I think we found ourselves some fancy drapes,' Wes replied and pointed to a small neat house to his left.

'I'd sure count them as fancy,' Dale replied.

'Never seen flowers like them afore,' Wes added. 'C'mon, let's scout round the back.'

Cautiously, the two men made their way down the side of the building until they rounded the back of what they assumed was Luther Parry's place.

First off, Wes tried the back door. It gave.

'I'll be danged,' he sighed. 'It ain't locked!'

Slowly, Wes eased the door open. The shrill screech from the hinges made both men cringe; in the silence of the night the sound was amplified.

Wes held the door where it was and listened for any sounds of movement from within.

There were none.

Cautiously, Wes continued to ease the door open until it was wide enough to enter.

Their eyes, now night-accustomed, took in the small kitchen they had entered. Wes put a finger to his lips as they moved forward to an open door at the far end of the room.

They found themselves in a small hallway with two closed doors: one to the left, the other to the right.

Wes and Dale paused, then Wes

decided on the left-hand door.

Gripping the handle he pushed it down and both men entered the room. Wes, his gun out, raced to the far side of the bed, where Luther Parry slept beside his wife. Dale reached out and clamped his hand across Parry's wife's mouth. Her startled eyes snapped open as he did so.

Wes, meanwhile, pulled the hammer back on his Colt and pressed the barrel into Luther Parry's face.

'Don't make a sound,' Wes warned.

Parry's mouth opened, but not a sound emerged from it.

Scanning his eyes round to his wife, he caught sight of the other man, a hand clamped firmly over his wife's mouth.

Turning his eyes back to Wes he stuttered, 'W-what do you w-want?'

'Easy now, friend,' Wes crooned. 'Do as you're told and no one will get hurt. Got it?'

Parry nodded.

'Tie her to that chair, yonder,' Wes

instructed Dale. 'And make sure she's gagged good and proper.'

Dale nodded and pulled Parry's wife from the bed.

'Now,' Wes turned his attention to Luther, 'we're gonna take a walk to the bank. You'll open it up, open the safe, and we take the money. Simple, see?'

'I-I don't have the combination or key for the safe. Only Mr Klugg has that, honest.'

Wes pressed the Colt's barrel harshly into Parry's face. 'You joshin' me?' he said.

'Mister, I promise you I'm tellin' the truth. Mr Klugg don't trust no one with that combination, not even me.'

'How you trading then?' Wes asked.

'We got a small float, and any monies paid in are stored in a steel drawer.'

'You got the key to that?'

'Yes, sir.'

Wes paused for a short while, then glanced across at Dale.

'She good and tight?' he asked.

'Sure thing, W — '

Wes glared at Dale but didn't say anything. Dale got the message, and looked down sheepishly under Wes's steely look.

'OK. Here's what we do — '

* * *

Clay reached the livery stables undetected. It was darker here, the livery being shielded from the moon's rays by the nearby saloon.

He paused at the double doors, pressing his ear against the small gap between the doors. He could hear hoofs scuffling the straw and the occasional snort from the horses, but no other movement.

He pulled at the doors but they wouldn't budge.

Damn! he thought, *Locked from the inside!*

That could only mean one thing: the liveryman slept on the premises. That could complicate things. But Clay didn't have the time to dawdle, he had to get to the horses.

Running round the side of the building, Clay looked for alternative ways into the stables. At the rear he found exactly what he hoped to find; a half-open window,

Looking round he found a crate. Standing on it, he managed to heave himself up and through the window into the dark interior.

Silent he was not. Going in head first, he landed with his head in a leather pail. He swung round and his legs kicked out, catching a harness hanging from the wall, which clattered to the stone floor.

Clay lay perfectly still, holding his breath and listening for any sound.

He lay there for what seemed like hours, but was only a few minutes. He heard nothing.

Getting to his feet he peered into the gloom to see where he was.

Then he felt the prod in his back.

'Hold it right there, mister!' a gravelly voice ordered.

Clay stood stock still. 'Easy, partner, I'm only here to collect our horses. Remember? We stabled 'em yesterday.'

'Turn round, real slow like,' the livery man's voice grated out.

Clay turned to face the man. The liveryman was holding a broomstick.

'Hell, man!' Clay almost shouted. 'You dang near give me a heart attack!'

'What the hell ya sneakin' around fer?' the liveryman asked, still holding the broom.

'Didn't want to wake anyone up,' Clay answered.

'How come ya lightin' out at this time o' the mornin'?'

'Couldn't sleep, so we decided to move on.'

'Seems mighty strange to me, young fella.'

'Well, that's the way of it,' Clay replied. 'Now I gotta saddle up the horses, so you get back to sleep, old-timer.'

'You saddlin' all three mounts?'

'I am.'

'Where's the other two then?'

'You ask too many damn questions!' Clay walked off towards the stalls and began to get their tackle together. He knew he had no choice now but to do something about the liveryman. He'd put two and two together pretty soon.

Clay couldn't allow that.

He'd saddled up two horses when he felt the eyes of the old man bore into him.

'You got nothin' better to do?' Clay said.

'Somethin's goin' down here, boy. What's the real reason fer all this sneakin' around, mister?'

Clay adjusted his Stetson and took a step towards the liveryman, smiled, and said: 'Well, to be honest, we're figurin' on robbin' the bank.'

At first the liveryman grinned, showing stained yellow teeth from years of chewing tobacco. But the grin faded as Clay drew his Colt.

'You plannin' on shootin' me?' The

liveryman showed no sign of panic or alarm.

Clay didn't answer. He knew he couldn't fire the gun; that would probably raise the sheriff at least, and their plans would be in ruins.

Clay gripped the Colt by the barrel, butt forward, then took a mighty swing at the liveryman, catching him just behind the ear.

The liverman fell to floor in a heap. Blood was already oozing from the head wound. He lay perfectly still.

Clay stood over him for a few moments, pondering his next move. Better hide the old man, he thought to himself.

Holstering his gun, Clay grabbed the man under his armpits and began dragging the body to the far end of the stables. He'd seen an empty stall there that would be ideal.

He laid the liveryman out in the corner of the stall and began to drag some hay to cover him. The old man had not moved.

Kneeling, Clay put his ear to the man's chest.

Shit! he thought. *He ain't breathin'!*

Clay stood. He tried to control the panic rising inside him. He'd never killed a man before.

Taking deep breaths, he calmed himself down, quickly covering the body with more straw. Then he grabbed an old tarp that was hanging near the stall and covered the dead man completely.

Quickly now, he saddled the third horse and, grabbing the reins of all three in his left hand, led them to the front of the livery stables.

The huge double doors were held by an iron bar across them. There was no lock, so they were easy to open. Breathing easier now, he calmly led the three animals out into the darkness of the alleyway.

*   *   *

Wes checked the rope and the gag that tied Parry's wife to the rocking-chair set

24

in the corner of the room.

'What's her name?' Wes asked Parry.

'Lucy,' Parry replied.

'Listen up, Lucy,' Wes began. 'We ain't aimin' to hurt you or your husband. As long as he does as he's told everything'll be all right. You understand?'

Wide blue eyes stared up at Wes Brown as the woman nodded vigorously.

'Now don't you fret none, ma'am, everything will be all right.'

Tears seeped from the woman's eyes as she looked pleadingly first at Wes, then her husband.

'I'll be back before you know it,' Luther said. 'Don't worry, my love.'

'C'mon,' Wes snapped. 'Let's get this show on the road.'

Dale pulled Parry to his feet.

'Can I at least get dressed?' Parry asked.

Surprisingly, neither Wes nor Dale had noticed the man was clothed only in a nightgown.

'Sure, but make it snappy.' Wes nodded.

Quickly, fingers trembling, Luther Parry pulled on a pair of pants, shook off the nightgown and donned a shirt. He then grabbed his boots from beneath the bed and slipped them on.

'Ready,' he said.

'OK, let's go,' Wes commanded.

With a look at his wife, Luther Parry gave her a reassuring smile. 'Be back soon, honey,' he said, and the three men left the room.

Outside, Wes turned to Dale. 'Follow me. I'll make sure no one is about. You keep Parry good and close. OK?'

'Sure thing W — '

A withering look stopped Dale in mid-sentence.

'Sorry. OK, we'll follow.'

Main Street was still deserted but darker now as clouds rolled in from the east obscuring the moon.

The wind was rising; small dust clouds were springing up from the parched earth, bone-dry after months of no rainfall, and beginning to sting their eyes.

Wes and Dale raised their bandannas to cover their mouths and peered through the gloom with slitted eyes. Luther Parry had no such luxury. He clasped his hand over his mouth to keep as much dust and grit out of his face as he could.

As quickly as it had started, it stopped.

The wind died down and the street became clear again. But in the distance, a rumble of thunder, faint at the moment, echoed.

A storm was nearing: just what Wes needed.

'Come on,' he whispered, 'the way ahead is clear. Bank's yonder.'

Suddenly Wes halted and raised an arm.

He turned his head, listening intently, and took out his Colt.

He'd heard the sound of hoofs before he saw the horses. He reholstered. 'It's Clay,' he mouthed. 'He's got the horses.'

By the time the three men reached

the bank, Clay had tethered the horses to the hitch rail, and was mopping his brow with a bandanna as Wes reached him.

'You OK, Clay? You seem a tad peaky,' Wes asked.

'Had a bit of trouble over to the livery. The owner lived on site. I killed a man, Wes.'

Wes was quiet for a moment before replying: 'Clay, can we talk about this later? I'm sure you did what you had to do. But right now we've got this bank at our mercy. Let's get this done and get outa this town, OK?'

'Sure. Sure, Wes. I'm OK, don't worry.'

'All right then. You stay and keep a lookout. Be ready to ride when we come out. OK?'

'OK.'

Wes grabbed the three saddle-bags. Two of them were empty; the third contained eight sticks of dynamite and fuses, brought just in case.

'Parry, get this here door open, now!'

Luther Parry fished out a bunch of keys, walked to door of the bank and inserted one into the lock. He pushed the door open and he, along with Wes and Dale, walked in.

'Close and lock the door,' Wes said.

Inside, the bank was very plain. Bare wooden walls, not a sign of any decoration. A counter ran three-quarters of the way across the rear of the bank; next to that was the manager's office. There were no chairs in the public area, just a small table upon which rested a pen and an inkpot.

The door leading to the tellers' station was locked, Parry used another key to unlock it, and all three passed through.

Each teller's station had a high-backed chair. They had three drawers each, and the counter also had pens and inkpots.

'Sure don't go in for no luxury,' Dale commented.

'Where's this metal drawer?' Wes demanded.

Again, Parry sorted through the keys, then walked to the far end of the counter. He inserted the key into what looked like another wooden drawer, but in fact it was only faced in wood.

Parry slid the heavy drawer open as Wes and Dale peered into it.

Dale whistled. 'Phew, that's a nice mess o' money,' he said, scooping up a handful of ten-dollar bills.

'How much is there?' Wes turned to Parry.

'No more'n four thousand,' Parry replied.

Again, Dale whistled. 'Most amount of money I ever did see,' he commented.

'Get it stashed in one of the saddle-bags,' Wes ordered, and Dale did so with pleasure.

'Now, where's the safe?' he asked Parry.

Without answering, Parry walked back across the bank to the far side and unlocked yet another door. He swung it open to reveal the manager's office.

The contrast with the bank's public area was astounding. A thick, plush red carpet covered the floor from wall to wall. A mahogany desk with two ornate oil lamps on either side stood in the middle of the room. A fancy pen-and-quill set was in the middle behind a wooden nameplate, the name painted in what looked like real gold: *Mr Seth Klugg, manager.*

A row of wooden filing cabinets stood to the left of the desk on either side of a curtained and barred window. On the facing wall stood a huge bookcase, ornately carved, holding more books than either Dale or Wes had seen outside of a library. Next to that stood a drinks cabinet. No drinks were on view, but there was an empty crystal decanter with matching crystal wineglasses and crystal tumblers.

The walls were covered in a heavy wallpaper and various portraits, presumably of bank officials, hung in profusion.

No sign of any family portraits, or

indeed, anything of a personal nature.

Tucked away in the far corner was the safe.

Dale made for it. 'Jeez,' he muttered, 'ain't never seen no safe as fancy as this before.'

'How many safes you seen?' Wes asked.

'Including this one?' Dale said.

'Yup.'

'Just the one.' Dale grinned.

Wes ignored the attempt at humour.

'You sure you ain't got no keys for this here safe?' he asked Parry.

'My word of honour, mister,' Parry replied. 'If I had it, and the combination, I'd give it to you. But I swear to God, Mr Klugg is the only one with that knowledge.'

Luther Parry was visibly shaking now. 'No amount of money is worth the life of my wife.'

Wes Brown believed the man. 'Hell, we ain't fixin' on killin' no one, 'specially a lady. So don't worry none on that score. But we are gonna blow this safe if we don't get the key and combination. When does this Klugg fella get back here?'

'Well, he's due back later today. Bank don't open on a Saturday or Sunday, 'less there's a drive, an' we ain't due one of them for a while.'

'So no one will expect the bank to open today?' Wes said. An idea was forming in his head and his face became animated.

'OK, Mr Parry, you sit yourself down in that there chair. Dale, see if you can find something to tie him with, and a gag.'

'I can't sit there, that's Mr Klugg's chair, he'd — '

'I said, sit!' Wes ordered.

Parry almost ran across the room to comply and sat, awkwardly, in the manager's chair.

Dale found rope and a some material for a gag.

When Parry was secure, Wes beckoned Dale to follow him out of the office.

'What ya figurin', Wes?' Dale asked, his expression perplexed.

'I figure we got two clear days afore the bank opens up again. If we stay put until this Klugg fella shows up, we can open the safe and ride out of here long before anyone gets suspicious. What d'ya think?'

'Sounds a bit risky, Wes. We don't even know if this Klugg fella is gonna show up here till Monday opening, so what then?'

'Well, in that case we give him till late Sunday, then we blow the safe as planned.'

'We better go see Clay, then, see what he thinks,' Dale said.

'OK. You keep your eye on Parry an' I'll go and explain the change of plan to Clay.'

* * *

Outside, Clay was getting edgy. He figured it was still a good three hours to sunrise, but the silence from inside the

34

bank was getting to him.

So when Wes came out of the bank, Clay almost jumped out of his skin.

'Jeez, Wes! What's going on?'

Wes then told Clay the change of plan. Clay listened intently, then slowly nodded.

'Get the horses back to the livery, unsaddle them, then join us here. OK?'

3

Clay led the three animals back to the livery stables. Apprehension filled him as he neared the double doors. There was a dead man inside. A dead man he'd killed.

Slowly, he pulled the doors open wide enough to get the animals inside, then quickly he closed and barred it. He'd leave the same way he got in.

He got the horses into their stalls, put a feed bag over the heads of each of them, then unsaddled them. The horses were restless to begin with, but the rich smell of oats calmed them and made his job easy.

Satisfied that all was well, and more than eager to get out of the livery, Clay reached the window and landed back in the dark alleyway. Relieved, he made sure the window was easily opened before making his way back to the bank.

It was Dale who let him in, quickly closing the door behind him.

'We already done got this,' Dale said, opening the saddle-bag and showing Clay the contents.

'Hot dog!' Clay said. 'How much is there?'

'Parry said about four thousand dollars.'

'A man could sure live the high life on that,' Clay said.

'A man could, but I doubt it'd last long with three men,' Dale said.

'Everything OK, Clay?' Wes asked.

'Yeah, sure. Locked the stable doors and made sure the back window was easy to open for when we go back.'

'Good thinkin', Clay. Now, we do have a small problem. Mrs Parry!'

'Hell, you ain't thinkin' of k — '

'God no! I only mean we can't leave her trussed up there for nearly two days. Someone might come acallin' and the game would be up.'

'What you suggestin'?' Dale asked.

'Go get her, and bring her here. That way we can keep an eye on them both,' Wes said.

'Makes sense, I guess,' Dale said. 'OK, I'll go get her. It's still dark and the town's abed, so it should be OK.'

'Keep the gag on, Dale,' Wes said. 'Don't want her ahollerin' fit to wake the dead.'

Dale grinned. 'I will, don't worry.'

* * *

Dale arrived at the Parry house without encountering a soul. It seemed like the whole town was dead.

He entered through the still-unlocked back door and walked to the parlour where, much to his surprise, Lucy Parry was asleep.

Although the room was pitch black, Dale stood silently and looked at the woman. He hadn't taken much notice of her when they first burst in, but now, he could see what a beauty she was. *How the hell did Luther Parry, a nondescript, plain-looking, skinny hombre, manage to get her?* he wondered.

Her pale, creamy skin showed an ample cleavage above her nightdress, her faultless complexion seemed to glow even in the murky light. Her long, brown, sleep-tangled hair had a lustre to it that gleamed.

Dale sighed. If he'd ever met and married a woman like her, he'd, well, he wouldn't be trying to rob a bank, for a start.

He gently shook a bare shoulder; the feel of her skin on his fingers sent an electric shot charging through him. A shock he did his best to ignore.

Her large blue eyes fluttered open, bewildered to start with, then anxious, then terrified.

'Don't fret none, ma'am,' Dale said in a low, husky voice that surprised him. 'Everythin's OK, just a change of plan is all. I'm gonna walk you down to the bank, you can be with your husband there, and you'll see that he's fine and dandy.

'It's just we couldn't leave you here for a couple of days, in case you had a caller.' Dale smiled at the woman, and some of her fear seemed to evaporate.

'I'm gonna untie you, but the gag stays. Sorry about that, but I gotta be certain sure you don't make a sound. OK?'

She nodded. Inside, she felt a sense of relief and instinctively knew this man meant her no harm.

As gently as he could, Dale untied the ropes and helped Lucy to stand.

She stood awkwardly at first, letting the blood flow to her legs and feet. She rubbed at her wrists to ease where the ropes had dug in.

'Sorry if'n they were too tight, ma'am,' Dale offered. He suddenly removed his Stetson and held it in both hands in front of him. 'We better get goin' now,' he added.

Lucy nodded. Dale held an arm out

to indicate that they should leave by the back door.

It didn't take long to reach the bank. Again, Main Street was deserted, but Dale kept to the shadows. The wind was rising and thunder again rumbled, far off but it was surely heading this way.

Dale knew that pretty soon the fine dust and hard-packed dirt that made up Main Street would turn to deep mud making travel difficult.

He knocked gently on the bank's door; it was opened by Clay who quickly ushered them in.

'Take her through to the office,' Wes said, 'make sure she's secured.'

'We're in for a long wait,' Clay said.

* * *

Seth Klugg was feeling mighty good about himself. He'd visited four ranchers in the vicinity who didn't yet bank with him and had three positive responses. Dollar signs were lighting up his eyes as he washed and dressed in the small hotel in Dewsburg.

Being an early bird, the sun hadn't risen yet, but he was eager to get home and then get to the bank to start the paperwork needed for his prospective clients.

It was a three-hour ride back to Springfield, a storm was brewing and Klugg was keen to get back as quickly as possible.

He had open terrain to cross with very little cover and he had no wet-weather gear, for which he silently cursed himself. But then, the weather had been fine when he had left Springfield, with no hint of what was to come.

Klugg finished packing his few possessions into his saddle-bag. He donned his frock-coat, then his Stetson; the last thing he put on was his gunbelt with holstered Smith & Wesson. He checked each of the chambers, making sure the one beneath the hammer was empty.

A safety precaution he'd learned after watching a cowboy dismount and shoot himself in the foot.

He'd never fired the gun, but felt somehow safer wearing it.

After taking a final look around the sparsely furnished room, then looking under the bed, he was satisfied he had everything and left nothing behind.

He slung his saddle-bag across one shoulder and made his way downstairs and on to the livery to collect his horse. The sun was just rising as he walked down the dusty street, but the scudding clouds flitting across the sky obscured most of the light.

He slipped the stable boy a dime to saddle up for him, mounted and set off for Springfield.

★   ★   ★

Unseen by Klugg, two pairs of eyes watched him as he cantered down the street.

The two men, shabbily dressed,

covered in trail dust and unshaven, silently watched the figure they hated.

Behind them, two nags waited patiently. In better times, the two trail-worn ponies would have been either put out to pasture, or ended up in a glue factory. But times weren't better.

The two horses, as well as their sidearms and battered Winchester rifles, were all the two men possessed.

They didn't have a pot to piss in.

The two men watched the cause of their present predicament ride out of town; as soon as he was out of sight they mounted their weary ponies and set off.

They figured they had two advantages over Klugg: surprise and the darkness, and they were determined to use those advantages.

Coming across Klugg had been a stroke of luck. They'd seen him ride in to the Bar X, where they'd just been hired to help with some branding work. It didn't take either man long to realize that fate had played a part in this, given them the opportunity to get even — at long last.

The men had been neighbours, each owning a smallholding, supplying Springfield with fresh vegetables, as well as a few of the outlying ranches.

Individually their properties were too small to worry the cattlemen, but when they started to consider that there were over thirty such smallholdings, some raising chickens, others pigs, and a few were even raising sheep, they soon realized that that was a lot of potential cattle country.

It didn't take long to get the bank, *their* bank, to start the foreclosures.

But Klugg had other plans. Foreclose he did, but the resale of the properties was kept a secret. A secret known only to himself and Enright. No money had changed hands; they both figured on paying when the railroad paid them.

It was all done legally and above-board with no gunplay or loss of life.

Just the loss of dignity, pride and livelihood.

Almost all the smallholders were married, some with small children; they had no alternative but to head for pastures new and put this part of their lives behind them.

But Jed Perkins and Silas Vance had no family, no ties, no responsibilites. They stayed around, looking for whatever work they could find.

Although it was unspoken between the two men, they both harboured a deep hatred of the Cattlemen's Bank, but most of all, a hatred of Seth Klugg.

Klugg had treated both men disdainfully, all but smiling as he told them to pay back their loans or mortgages within twenty-four hours or vacate their land. This, of course, was impossible.

Now fate had given the two men a chance to get their own back.

Walking their ponies out of town, they followed Klugg. They knew his route; there was only one sensible route from Dewsburg to Springfield, and they had a few hours in which to make their move.

And make it they would.

Their plan was simple, they'd cut across open country and get ahead of Klugg to set their ambush.

Then they'd kill him.

They followed at a leisurely pace for perhaps twenty minutes before they left the trail and headed east, knowing that, although it meant rougher ground to cover, it was a short cut that rejoined the main trail around four miles ahead.

The sun was over the eastern horizon by now, but its dull red glow hardly shed any light. The dark clouds, ominous now, and the rolls of thunder following upon the lightning flashes, were ever closer.

Soon the rain would fall.

Jed and Silas reined in and dismounted, ground-hitching their ponies out of sight of the trail. They each reached for their Winchester rifles and made sure they were loaded. Then they made their way to the trail. There was little cover closer to the trail, so they were both grateful for the weak light.

Neither man had spoken since they'd left Dewsburg, but Silas turned to Jed as they lay flat on the ground. 'Best we shoot first; no point takin' any risks.'

'Sure, I just want him dead!' Jed replied.

'Shouldn't be too long now; that short cut saves two or three miles on the trail.'

No sooner had he uttered the words than they heard the soft patter of hoofs on sand. Silhouetted against a red-black sky, they saw the lone horseman approaching.

His mount was at an easy walk; obviously the rider was in no particular hurry, or else he was giving his mount a breather. Either way, Jed and Silas raised their rifles to their shoulders.

Taking deep breaths, fingers on the trigger and sighting down the long barrels, both men fired simultaneously.

At first, and only for an instant, Seth Klugg thought the thunder was getting closer. The roar of both rifles rang out across the silent prairie and, before he knew it, a slug hit him in the right shoulder, spinning him round and throwing him to the ground.

The horse reared and set off in a panicked gallop as Klugg lay on the ground, trying to come to his senses, wondering what the hell was going on.

Shock was a strange partner. Seth as yet felt no pain, it took him a few seconds even to realize he'd been shot.

When he did, the pain set in. But he wasn't dead, nor was he willing to go down with a whimper.

With his rifle still in its scabbard on the bolting horse, all he was left with was his Smith & Wesson revolver. He had no idea where the shots had come from or how far away they were.

Were they within his range? Or had they used rifles? If the latter, he assumed they were out of range.

Being left-handed, the shoulder wound didn't hinder him. Slowly, cautiously, he moved his left hand to the butt of his six-gun and gently pulled it clear of leather, cocking the hammer at the same time.

He could feel the warm trickle of blood running down his right arm, but could do nothing to stem it. He just had to wait, be patient, and hope the bushwhacking sons of bitches came to inspect their cowardly work.

Minutes passed, and Klugg was beginning to wonder if they would ever show themselves. His right arm and hand were getting numb, but he could still feel the blood.

He was lying awkwardly: a stone was digging into the small of his back and his right leg was tucked under his left leg, bent at the knee. He didn't think it was broken, but his right foot was feeling numb too.

Pain raced through Klugg's body, but he was determined to remain still and bide his time. He wasn't ready to die just yet.

Jed and Silas had also not moved a

muscle. Jed whispered, 'Can you see him?'

'Just about,' Silas replied. 'Ain't seen him move though.'

'No, me neither. Should we go check, ya think?'

'Dunno, might be playin' possum.'

Jed pondered this.

'Damn sure one of us hit him. No one falls off a horse like that 'lessen they was hit.' Jed looked to Silas. 'Maybe he's dead?'

'OK, let's see if we can make him move a tad,' Jed said.

With that, he raised the rifle to his shoulder and squinted down the sight. Jed, like Silas, was a good shot with a rifle: they had to be, hunting down game was the only way to provide meat.

He levered a slug into the breech and gently squeezed the trigger.

★ ★ ★

Back at the bank, Wes Brown was pacing the floor of the manager's office.

Luther and Lucy were in one corner of the room, and only had eyes for each other, but both seemed a mite calmer now they were together.

Wes reached a decision, part based on hunger and thirst, and part based on providing a sense of normality. He addressed Dale and Clay.

'Reckon you two should head back to the roomin'-house for a spell,' he said.

This caught both men by surprise.

'What?' Dale asked.

'Well, I figure that this Klugg fella might be a while yet, an' if none of us is seen about, it might raise suspicion, 'specially as our horses are still in the livery, along with a dead liveryman.' He turned to Luther. 'There a back way outa here?'

Luther nodded: he looked at his wife before he tilted his head at the far side of the office and looked towards the side wall.

Puzzled, Wes crossed the room to take a closer look.

There was a bookcase fixed to the wall. Wes looked quizzically at Luther.

Again Luther nodded.

'Well I'll be danged,' Wes said. 'A hidden door. How's it open?'

Luther, gagged, couldn't answer.

'I'm gonna lower the gag so you can tell me, but one false sound and this here gun butt will come down so hard you might never wake up. Understand?'

Luther nodded vigorously.

Wes lowered the gag.

'See the small green book to the right, middle shelf?'

Wes nodded.

'That's the handle. Just pull and twist and the door will open. You'll hear a small click as the lock is released.'

Wes replaced the gag and walked back to the bookcase.

He took hold of the green book, pulled and twisted to the left.

Nothing happened.

He turned to Luther, who shook his head to the right. Wes took the hint and tried again.

He turned the book to the right and the door opened.

'I'll be,' Dale said. 'That's some fancy door all right. Never even give that there bookcase a second glance.'

'OK, that's your way out. Now, get back to the room, make yourselves seen if anyone's about, then when the café opens get us some grub and coffee. If anyone asks after me, tell 'em I got a bug, so I'm eatin' in the room. That way there'll be no awkward questions. And make sure that Ma Dooley don't interfere. Got that?'

'Sure, I ain't stupid,' Dale answered, sounding aggrieved. Already he was having second thoughts about the whole venture. It went against the grain and his conscience was bothering him.

Folks had seemed pretty friendly and the town had a good feeling to it.

Maybe he should try and talk them out of —

His thoughts were interrupted as Wes, their unelected leader, went on:

'When you get back, knock three

times so I know it's you. But make sure the alleyway is empty so no one sees you.'

'It's Sunday,' Clay said. 'Most folks'll be either in the church or the saloon.'

Cautiously, Wes opened the door a little further, conscious of the creaking hinges, and peered into the back alleyway.

It was still encased in shadow; he could neither hear nor see any sign of movement.

'OK, get going.'

4

The bullet from Jed's Winchester caught Klugg's outstretched right foot. The pain was instant and excruciating, and he lost conciousness.

'He move any?' Silas asked.

'Well his foot sure did,' Jed replied.

'Let's go take us a looksee, but keep that rifle ready, just in case.'

Both men got to a crouching position, rifle at hip level.

Keeping low, they edged forward, ready to fling themselves flat at the slightest movement from their victim.

There was none.

They moved ever closer. Both men saw the small stains of blood that spread onto the sand, one by the shoulder and the second by his foot.

Klugg's eyes fluttered open. He felt no pain, he was well past that now as his brain tried to save his body.

He was aware of movement near by and, still clutching his Smith & Wesson tightly, he waited.

Within seconds forked lightning raked the ground, briefly illuminating the scene. A clap of thunder roared that seemed to be directly overhead. It was so loud that the very earth shook.

The lightning flashed again and again, which to Klugg made a surreal picture as he caught sight of the two men approaching.

It was enough to give him a fix. He was going to go down fighting.

Jed and Silas stood rock still. The thunder and lightning, unexpected as it was, had momentarily taken them off-guard.

It gave Klugg the chance he'd been waiting for. He raised the barrel of his revolver, guessing both trajectory and position, and squeezed the trigger.

Nothing! Damn! The empty chamber. He quickly thumbed back the hammer and squeezed the trigger again. This time the gun fired its lethal load.

At the same time, Silas, seeing the movement, let loose with his Winchester.

Silas Vance stood erect. The .44 from Klugg's Smith & Wesson caught him in the throat, exiting from the back of his neck.

It seemed as if his head exploded in a fountain of blood, and Jed turned sideways as it showered him.

The impact of the bullet was dissipated somewhat as it passed clean through, leaving Silas still standing for almost a minute before he crumpled to the ground.

Dead.

Seth Klugg made one fatal mistake. As he lifted his Smith & Wesson, he also raised his head. No more than two inches, but enough for Silas's bullet to take the top of his head off. The slug hit him just above the eyes and his brain, blood and splinters of bone were sent gushing across the dry earth.

Jed Perkins was in a state of shock. The horrors he'd just witnessed were unprecedented in his experience.

He sank to his knees and vomited the entire contents of his stomach.

And then some.

Trying hard to pull himself together, Jed looked at his long-time friend. They'd got their revenge, but at what price?

'I'm sorry, partner,' he mumbled. 'It weren't worth this.'

What to do? What to do? Jed's brain raced, he had to get his act together. He couldn't leave Silas's body out here to be carrion fodder; he owed him that much.

Jed walked back to the horses; they were agitated, he could tell, the smell of blood was in the air.

He led both horses back to Silas's body. Retrieving a bedroll, he carefully wrapped Silas in it and hefted the body onto Silas's pony.

Klugg could stay where he was, no way was he gonna give that rat a decent burial.

The horses ground-hitched, Jed walked

to Klugg's body. Even in his state of grief and shock, Jed's lips parted in a gruesome grin. 'Rot in hell, Klugg, cos that's where you're surely headed.'

Jed turned, then paused.

Klugg's horse! The nag would probably make it back to town, and then what? They'd *know* something had happened. That would alert the sheriff.

Taking down his saddle-bag, Jed walked back to the body and began going through Klugg's pockets.

'No sense in leaving you with earthly possessions,' he thought.

He put Klugg's Smith & Wesson in his belt and began to search his pockets. He found some loose change in his trouser pockets, a wallet, stuffed with tens and twenties: that would come in handy, Jed thought. And a whole bunch of keys was clipped to his belt. He stuffed the money into his saddle-bags but left the keys, and stood up.

Casting a final glance at the now

ex-bank manager, he felt tempted to kick the body, but refrained.

Klugg's eyes were wide open. His jaw was set in a macabre silent scream.

Then the rain came. Dollar-sized drops hit the dry earth, sending mini dust clouds up for a few brief moments before the dust gave way to a cloying sticky mud. The rain was so heavy, the ground had no time to soak it up and surface water started to form.

Lightning struck and thunder clapped almost simultaneously.

Jed knew he had to get away from here and find some cover. He donned a tarp cape over his head, securing it with a rope, and mounted up. Leading Silas's pony, he set off back towards Dewsburg. He'd figure what to do as he travelled.

★   ★   ★

The rain, hitting the tin roof of the bank, sounded like a Gatling gun to those inside.

61

The sudden onslaught made Lucy jump.

'Only rain, ma'am,' Wes assured her.

Wes walked though the bank to the front door and risked a peek outside.

Although it was just after nine, dark clouds all but obliterated any light the early-morning sun might have shed. There was enough light to see across the street: he watched as the rain turned the dry, dusty ground to a morass of mud.

He walked back to the manager's office just as he heard three knocks on the secret door.

He took out his Colt, turned the green book and pulled the door open just enough to make sure it was Dale and Clay.

Both men wore tarp capes, water gushed from their Stetsons. 'Let us in,' Dale said.

Wes pulled the door open and the two dripping men came in. They took off their hats, rubbed water from their eyes, and shook excess water from the tarps.

Beneath Clay's tarp was a basket, and Wes could smell bacon.

'Hot damn,' Dale said, 'that rain is full of hail, too. I never seen anything like that storm. Town's awash.'

'Never mind that,' Wes said, 'let's eat, I'm starving!'

'We got bacon, bread, coffee and water,' Clay said as he put the basket on the manager's desk.

Wes removed the napkin covering the food, grabbed some bread and slices of still-hot bacon, and stuffed them into his mouth.

'My, that sure is welcome,' he said, his mouth full and crumbs and fat circling his lips.

Dale got out five tin mugs and poured the freshly brewed coffee into them.

'Now, if you two folks wanna eat,' Dale said, 'you gotta give your word not to try anything funny.'

Luther Parry nodded, his stomach rumbling. Lucy lowered her head.

'OK, gonna untie ya fer a while.

Cover 'em, Clay.'

Clay took out his Colt.

Dale brought the steaming mugs of coffee over, then made them each a bacon sandwich. He took out two plates and handed them one apiece.

'Ain't no one foolish enough to be out and about in that rain,' Clay said. 'Never seen rain that heavy.'

Silence descended as the group ate and savoured the coffee.

The silence was broken by Lucy.

'What do you intend doing with us, when . . . when this is over?' she said. Her sandwich remained untouched.

Wes swallowed the last of his food, and took a gulp of coffee to wash it down before answering.

'Ma'am, we mean you no harm; all we want is the money and we'll be outa here and outa your lives for ever. We ain't killers; hell, this is the first time we all been on the wrong side of the law.

'When this is over, we'll leave you here. You have my word.'

The conversation was cut short by

the sound of loud voices outside the bank.

They all froze.

'Gags!' Wes whispered. 'Get them gags back on.'

Hurriedly, Dale and Clay replaced the gags and retied both Luther and Lucy to the chairs.

'Dale, go see what the commotion's all about.'

Dale donned his cape and Stetson and left the office by the back door.

Wes and Clay had their pistols out, ready for anything that might happen.

Again Wes whispered, 'Keep your eyes on these two.' Carefully and slowly he almost tiptoed from the office and approached the bank's front door.

Leaning forward, Wes put his ear to the door. At first all he could hear were muffled voices; the rain made too much noise to pick up more than the odd word. But whatever was happening out there, folks seemed to be het up about it.

Wes returned to the office.

'What's goin' on?' Clay asked.

'Couldn't hear a damn thing,' Wes replied. 'Seems to be a lot of shouting but couldn't make out what the fuss is about.'

At that moment three knocks sounded on the back wall.

Wes rushed across the room to let Dale in.

'We got trouble,' Dale said, shaking water off his cape and taking his Stetson off. 'Klugg's horse just came in.'

'So?' Wes said.

'Klugg weren't on it!'

⋆   ⋆   ⋆

Sheriff Clint West had had a bad night.

He finished his rounds by ten that night, then made his way as he always did, to the Golden Horn.

A few beers before turning in and marking the end of another day.

Nothing much ever happened in Springfield. The occasional drunk; rowdy rannies

66

out blowing their month's wages on booze and, if they were lucky, a fallen dove for an hour or two. And his deputies did most of the work these days.

His conscience caught up with him now and then. He hated being the lackey for Enright. The extra pay was welcome, sure; the pittance he got for putting his life on the line was an insult.

West was stuck between Klugg and Enright, doing their bidding as and when they demanded. Running the homesteaders off land that was rightfully theirs went against the grain but he couldn't resist the money, nor the fact that his and Enright's paths had crossed a few years back in Denver.

West had been arrested after a bar-room brawl that had escalated to gunplay.

West could see that he was no match for the bull of a man who took exception to his very existence and had drawn his pistol with the intent of sideswiping the man. But in the ensuing struggle, the gun had gone off.

West had killed an unarmed man.

By pure chance, Enright was in the same saloon and had just, moments before, been arrested for cheating at a game of poker. It had been his luck that two of the players were, in fact, deputies on a night off and they soon cottoned on to Enright.

As soon as the blast of the gun shattered the evening, the deputies grabbed West, too, and marched both men down to the city jail.

There followed a catalogue of errors: the jail, purpose-built and housing twenty cells, was full to capacity with at least five men to each cell. Staffed by inexperienced and underpaid jailers, confusion reigned.

Within a matter of hours Enright saw a way of just plain walking out of the jail.

A lot of the prisoners were drunks, picked up merely to be fined after a night in the cells, increasing the revenue of the sheriff's office. And on such a busy Saturday night, Enright saw that some of the old hands merely called the jailer, offered to pay the fine and left.

Both men paid a fine and walked out. It was as simple as that.

West and Enright left Denver that night and teamed up, looking for pastures new.

Springfield turned out to be their new pasture.

Enright soon made a few bucks at the tables, while West figured on finding work on a ranch.

But fate had other ideas.

Coincidence seemed to follow the two men.

A fight broke out and guns were drawn. The two protagonists, from neighbouring ranches, far the worse for drink, were firing haphazardly at each other. People fell to the floor or tried to make it through the batwings — anywhere to get out of the random line of fire.

Two men were hit, one fatally.

Without thinking, Clint West floored one of the men with his gun butt, then he faced the other cowboy.

'Drop the gun, son,' he said in a menacing voice. 'You done fired off five shots, you sure there's another slug in there?'

The cowboy glared at West; he wasn't drunk enough to take a chance and he let the pistol fall to the floor.

'Someone get the sheriff,' West shouted out.

'Cain't do that, mister.'

'Why the hell not?'

'He's lyin' yonder, dead as a boulder.'

Clint let his eyes wander to the crumpled heap lying on the floor. The unlucky recipient of a .45 slug. The light from an oil lamp reflected off the tin star pinned to the man's vest.

'Ain't there no deputies?'

'Nope,' came the reply.

While West's attention was occupied elsewhere, the ranny whose slug had probably killed the sheriff went for his Bowie.

'Mister — !' voices rang out.

The ranny's actions were slowed by the beer and whiskey, and just as his knife came out of its scabbard, West shot.

The slug took the man plumb centre in the chest, his feet lifted off the floor and he was slammed against the saloon wall, where he seemed to slump in slow motion to the floor.

His chest was already covered in blood and it slowly spread across the floor.

Clint stood there with his smoking Colt gripped tightly; he expected trouble.

What he got took him by surprise.

From the far corner of the saloon, a man in dude's clothing was brushing the sawdust off his fancy jacket. He had bright-red hair and a similarly coloured wispy moustache set in a face that was almost as red. He raised a squeaky and somewhat nervous voice.

'Well, folks, looks like we got ourselves a new sheriff!'

A drunken roar went up as the man,

who happened to be the town's mayor, called, 'Drinks on the house!'

The stampede towards the bar was instant and Springfield had a new sheriff.

In the background, Wilbur Enright smiled.

* * *

The few beers turned into a lot of beers. What the hell, West thought, I ain't even needed no more in this goddamn town anyways. Soon as the railroad comes and Klugg and Enright move in they'll run me outa here quicker than a gopher down a hole.

'Whiskey!' he shouted at the barkeep.

'You sure, Clint?' the 'keep asked.

'What, are you, my keeper?' Clint snarled. 'I said *whiskey*!'

The barkeep, who'd seen Clint in this mood many times before, knew when not to argue.

'One whiskey comin' up, Sheriff.' He slid a shot glass across the bar and Clint grabbed and downed it in one.

Wilbur Enright appeared by the sheriff's side as if by magic. 'Leave the bottle, Sam,' he said to the barkeep.

'On me, Sheriff,' Enright said in his patronizing voice.

Suddenly, West didn't feel like drinking any more. But nevertheless, he picked up the shot glass and downed another whiskey in one gulp.

'You seem a tad nervous, Clint,' Enright said. 'Somethin' bothering you?'

'No, no, Mr Enright, just got the rounds to finish off.'

'Well, don't let me keep you from your duty, Clint.'

'Thanks, Mr Enright, but I better leave now. Busy day tomorrow.'

He tipped his Stetson, made his excuses and left the saloon.

Enright watched him go on slightly unsteady legs and thought, *That man is nearing the end of his usefulness!*

5

The rapping on the sheriff's office door and the loud voice calling: 'Sheriff! *Sheriff!* You better come quick!' woke West up from his drunken slumber.

Groggily, he got to his feet and staggered to the door. He managed to pull back the bolt at the second attempt and a gust of rain-heavy wind hit him like a sledge-hammer.

'What the hell!' West yelled.

'Mr Klugg's hoss just hit town, and he ain't on it,' the man said, obviously excited.

'Goddamn, you woke me up fer that?'

The man seemed shocked. 'But Sheriff — '

'Get down to Luther's place an' tell him. Where's the horse now?'

'Outside the bank,' the man replied.

'OK, I'll get down there, now scoot.'

He slammed the door shut and made his way to the wash stand, poured water into a bowl and splashed his face. He managed to resurrect the smouldering logs in the pot-bellied stove and put the coffee pot on to boil. There was no way he could leave without his morning institution of strong, black Arbuckles'.

Although the thunderheads were moving westwards, the rain was falling heavier now. Main Street was already ankle-deep in mud as Clint West reluctantly left his office. Water dripped from his Stetson as he made his way to the bank.

A small knot of townsfolk were gathered around Seth Klugg's horse; speculation was rife.

'All right, move away,' West ordered as he reached the group. He inspected the horse, but in the half-light it was difficult to see if anything was amiss.

'Let's get this nag over to the livery so's I can inspect it in the dry,' he said to one of the men. 'Go rouse ol' Abe.'

A man ran off to get the livery open

as West grabbed the reins and began to walk the animal to the livery stable.

The townsman was still hammering on the stable door when West arrived. 'Can't seem to raise him, Sheriff,' he said.

West grunted, 'Hold these reins.'

The sheriff took his gun out and hammered on the door.

Still no response.

'There another way in?' he asked.

'I'll go check, Sheriff,' a volunteer offered.

West waited, thoroughly pissed off by now. He was cold, wet and hung over; this he did not need.

Then he heard movement from within the livery and the door creaked as it swung open, but it wasn't Abe who opened the door. It was the volunteer.

'Side window was open, Sheriff. Ain't seen no sign of Abe though.'

'Maybe he was on a bender last night,' West offered, unconcerned. 'Let's git a look at this horse.'

He led the animal inside, glad to be

out of the rain, took off his Stetson and cape and handed them to the man who'd opened up the livery. 'Let's get some light over here,' the sheriff ordered.

Oil lamps were lit and brought over and West began to check over the horse.

He ran his hands over the animal's neck, then its rump. Even after all the rain there were red stains on his hands. Blood had dried, and West thought something must have happened before the rain came.

There was a dark stain on the saddle. 'Looks like blood to me,' the sheriff said. 'Whatever happened to Klugg sure weren't no accident.'

'Sheriff!' a voice called out. 'You better get over here!'

'What now?'

'I jus' found Abe, Sheriff,' the man replied.

West led the horse to a stall and instructed someone to unsaddle and feed it, then he walked to the back of the livery.

Abe's body was half-buried under straw, a tarp had been pulled back to reveal his caved-in skull.

'Was the flies, Sheriff, whole bunch of 'em. Abe would never allow flies in here, the place was always spotless — for a livery, anyways.'

West knelt down to get a closer look at the fatal wound, as he did so, he felt his head throb. *Goddamn whiskey,* he thought.

'Who the hell would do this to ol' Abe?' a bystander asked. The question was rhetorical.

At that point two of the town's deputies showed up, Al Croop, a young and eager youth, and the more sober Jack Jimson, who harboured a desire to be sheriff. He had no time for Clint West, seeing the man for what he was, a lackey to Enright and Krugg.

'You two, find out who owns these horses. I wonder if Abe kept a record of his customers?' West asked.

'Doubt it, Sheriff. Far as I know ol'

Abe couldn't read nor write none,' a man said.

'You reckon these two incidents are linked, Sheriff?' Al Croop asked, his eyes alight with excitement.

'Always a possibility,' the sheriff replied. 'But I sure as hell can't see what would link 'em. Krugg is either injured or wounded out on the trail somewheres and Abe here, well, he got slugged in here, I reckon. See the blood yonder?'

West pointed to a spot some ten feet away. 'Looks like he was slugged over there and dragged into this stall,' the sheriff concluded.

A breathless man rushed into the livery. 'Sheriff, ain't no sign of Luther or his wife. I hammered an' hollered but no one's home. Went round the back and the door was open, so I went inside, but the house sure was empty.'

Sheriff Clint West stood to his full height and scratched his aching head in puzzlement.

'Reckon Luther did ol' Abe and then

got Klugg, Sheriff?' Croop suggested.

'Nah. Luther Parry wouldn't say boo to a goose,' Jack Jimson cut in.

'Well, he's the only link we got here,' West stated. 'Luther was in town, killed Abe and stole a horse, then bushwhacked Klugg out on the trail.'

'What in hell would Luther Parry do that for?

'That's what we gotta find out.'

'Shall we get a posse together, Sheriff?' Al asked expectantly.

'Search party, more like. We gotta find Klugg or the Parrys or both hopefully, see what we can piece together. Six men will be enough.'

'Right on it, Sheriff.' Al Croop was fired up as he left the livery.

* * *

Jed Perkins was stuck between a rock and a hard place. Or, to be more accurate, he was stuck on an island that had been created as the rain lashed down and a flash flood had almost overwhelmed him and his dead partner.

He'd made barely a mile down the old short cut and now wished he'd gone by the main trail.

The rain had started shortly after he'd loaded Silas onto his horse. He knew a storm was brewing, but the rain was only light. All he wanted to do was get clear of Klugg's body.

Jed sat under his tarp willing the rain to stop. He chewed on some jerky as the rain hit the tarp, sounding like a drum in his ears.

He'd ground-hitched both horses but they were still agitated; the dead body was bad enough, Jed knew they could smell blood, but the now-distant rumble of thunder and the odd flash of lightning didn't help.

The rain hadn't let up any, and the stream running either side of the small mound he'd managed to get to was slowly turning into a raging torrent of muddy water.

Jed stood and surveyed the area. He was completely surrounded by water.

He could see debris sweeping past: cactus, yucca, cottonwood branches, even rocks.

This didn't look good, he thought. He peered into the distance at the lowland hills and the mountain beyond. A strange noise filled his ears. A distant rumble that wasn't thunder.

'What in hell?' he thought, trying to focus, wiping the rain from his face.

The rumble grew louder: a roar that seemed to be all around him, yet in the grey light he could see nothing. The horses started whinnying, rearing on their hind legs, Jed could see they were now panicking, the whites of their eyes showing, their ears flat to their heads. They knew what was happening.

Then he saw it.

He stood stock still, unable to believe his eyes as the wall of debris-filled water hit him.

That was the last thing he ever saw.

★   ★   ★

82

'You two boys get back to the rooming-house,' Wes said. 'We gotta maintain an appearance. If'n folks don't see you around they might get suspicious.'

'Right, Wes,' Dale replied.

'An' make sure no one comes into the room, else they'll start askin' stupid questions as to where I am. Jus' keep up the story that I ain't feelin' so good, OK?'

'Sure thing. C'mon, Clay, we'll get ourselves some coffee and see what's goin' on out there.'

Wes opened the secret door for them and checked the alleyway was clear, then the two men left and Wes closed the door quietly.

Hitting Main Street, Dale and Clay walked casually, the rain was still heavy, but not as heavy as it had been.

Mud clung to their boots as they crossed the street and mounted the boardwalk, slippery with rain. They halted for a while, surveying the town. Mostly deserted, a few men scurrying from shelter to shelter in a fruitless attempt to stay dry.

The Golden Horn was already open for business; few had ventured out into the rain, but the stalwarts always did. It'd take an earthquake to stop the hardened drinkers from turning up.

There were about fifteen cowpokes in the saloon, most standing at the long wooden bar.

'What'll it be, gents?' the barkeep said, smiling.

'Coffee if'n ya got any,' Clay said, 'and some pie wouldn't go amiss.'

'Coming right up.' The 'keep left the bar unattended and walked into the rear kitchen, emerging a few moments later with two plates of pie and two mugs of steaming black coffee.

'Lot of excitement today, gents,' the 'keep said affably.

'How so?' Dale asked between mouthfuls of pie.

'Ain't ya heard? Seth Klugg's horse

came in an' no one was on it. Then over to the livery, they found ol' Abe dead as a doornail with his skull crushed in.'

'Jeez,' muttered Clay. 'They got any suspects yet?'

'Nah. Sheriff's getting a posse together to go look for Klugg, but that's about it. Oh, and the Parrys have gone amissin', too.'

'The Parrys?' Dale asked innocently.

'Luther Parry is the assistant manager. Him an' his wife just disappeared,' the 'keep replied. 'Say,' he suddenly added, 'weren't there another fella with you yesterday?'

'Yeah, he's got a stomach bug or somethin',' Dale answered. 'We left him to sleep.'

'Ain't ya gettin' the doc in?'

'Nah, he ain't that serious an' he don't like sawbones none too much, either.' Dale lit up a stogie.

'Cain't say I blame him fer that.' The 'keep grinned.

Al Croop burst into the saloon at that point. 'Sheriff's needing six men,' he hollered. 'Any volunteers?'

He eyed the men at the bar, expectantly.

Dale had a sudden brainwave. 'Here, I'll go,' he called across.

'You crazy?' Clay whispered.

'Think on it, Clay,' he replied. 'I can keep tabs on what's going down and, more importantly, no one will suspect any of us if'n we're helping out the sheriff.' He winked at Clay.

'Hot damn!' Clay said quietly. 'I get ya now.'

'What about you, mister?' Al asked.

Dale answered him. 'We got ourselves a sick partner, so Clay here had better keep an eye on him.'

'Oh, sure thing, mister. Well that's fair enough. Hope he ain't too ill.'

'Nah, he'll be fine, just needs rest and quiet,' Dale said.

'OK, be at the livery in five minutes. The rain's eased off a bit so we'll be riding out soon,' Al Croop said. He moved off heading towards the other cowboys in the saloon, who suddenly remembered they had other places to go.

Al left the saloon to continue his search for posse members.

'You be sure an' tell Wes what the plan is, Clay?'

'Will do, but I'll get back to the room first, make sure no one's been in.'

'Good idea, stay there till the posse rides out an' then git back to Wes.'

Dale stood. 'Better get over to the livery and saddle up.' He smiled.

The 'keep walked down the bar and said: 'Mighty decent of you, stranger, to lend a hand like that.'

'No problem,' Dale replied, 'We all gotta do our bit.' He looked round at the other men in the saloon, who avoided his eyes.

'Be seein' ya soon, *amigo*,' he said to the 'keep. Then turned to Clay and said in a louder voice, 'You make sure our partner is looked after, Clay.'

'I surely will.' Clay winked and both men left the bar.

* * *

The six-foot high wall of water and tree trunks that carried Silas's body, the two horses and Jed off had begun in the mountains.

What started out as small trickles of water ran down the steep slopes, forming streams, which became torrents. As they reached the foothills, the water was fed through ancient courses into a deep gorge, where it gushed in a boiling, swirling frenzy.

Slowly the gorge began to fill and as the rain continued to pour, the deadly barrage was released to continue its doomed journey downwards.

Jed was flung sideways as his legs were whipped from under him. For a while he rode the wave, gasping for breath every time his head bobbed above the surface. But the force of the water and the debris it contained eventually won.

Jed went under; he felt a sharp pain in his side as a jagged branch lanced him like a knife through butter. Small rocks pounded his body. A boot was ripped off his foot and his shirt was torn to shreds as he was finally engulfed.

His last look at life was through murky water, inches from the surface and his gaze fixed on a watery, dull sun.

His eyes bulged as he could no longer hold his breath, he let the remaining air out of his lungs and breathed in water.

It was then that he died.

Almost as quickly as it had started, the torrent dissipated as the weight of water behind the flood diminished.

Jed Perkins's semi-naked body lay in a foot of water, face down in mud.

By some miracle one of the ponies, badly injured, had survived. It struggled to its feet and stood, head bowed, breathing heavily.

It hadn't the strength to move, so it just stood there trembling.

The pony that held Silas's body was less fortunate. A foot-long gash in its belly had spilled its guts. It lay on one side, entrails gently floating in the now-placid water.

Of Silas, there was no sign. The force of the current had ripped the body from the pony and sent it tumbling onwards. It finished up wrapped round a giant cactus; of the bedroll he was wrapped in, only vague bits of cloth remained.

Even in death, it seemed Klugg had got his way.

6

Ma Dooley was brushing the hall floor when Clay entered.

He stopped dead in his tracks. His boots were coated in mud.

'Sorry, ma'am,' he said, removing his soaked Stetson. 'I didn't think.'

'Take your boots off in the porch, young man. Hard enough keepin' this place tidy.'

'Again, sorry, ma'am.'

Clay backed out through the door, sat on the porch chair and took his offending boots off. He placed them beside the chair and stood in his stockinged feet.

'Made some chicken soup for your friend,' she said.

'Thank you kindly, ma'am, I'll make sure he gets it. He seems a bit better today, all he needs is peace and quiet,' Clay said, hoping she'd get the message.

He knew from his experience with previous landladies how nosy they were.

'I'll go check on him now, ma'am,' Clay excused himself.

'Call me Ma, everybody does,' she said.

'OK, Ma,' he said, and climbed the short staircase to their room. He looked back once and, fortunately, Ma Dooley carried on with her brushing. He'd half-expected her to follow and he breathed a sigh of relief.

Unlocking the door, he entered the room, making sure to lock the door behind him. He threw his hat on to a small table, unbuckled his gun-rig and flopped down on the bed.

He'd stay about an hour, he thought, and closed his eyes.

* * *

The rain was easing up now, the wind was dropping and the black clouds overhead were getting lighter by the minute as Dale set off for the livery stables.

Then, on impulse, he made a slight detour to the general store. He suddenly realized he'd no idea how long he'd be gone or, indeed, where he would be heading and he had nothing with him for a journey of any description.

'Help you, mister?'

A woman in her later forties, Dale guessed, was behind a counter crammed with dry-goods and quite a lot of candy in glass jars.

'Howdy, ma'am,' Dale said, doffing his hat. 'I'm off to join the posse. No doubt you've heard there's been trouble, an' I realized I ain't got me no provisions.'

'You won't be needin' much,' the woman replied. 'Deputy Al Croop was just in an' he picked up a bunch o' stuff; town pays for that. You might need tobacco, if'n you smoke some, and maybe some jerky. Coffee, beans and ham are all supplied, mister.'

'Well, OK, I'll take a plug of tobacco, some papers and some of that fine-looking jerky, ma'am.'

'Jerky's on the house,' she told him. 'Abe was a good friend of mine. 'Sides, I make it myself and I guarantee you ain't never had jerky like it before.'

'Well thank you, ma'am, I sure hope we find whoever is behind all this. Oh, I better have a coupla boxes of lucifers, too.'

The woman got his provisions ready for him. He paid for the tobacco, papers and lucifers, which the woman had placed in a small sack, adding a generous amount of jerky wrapped in paper.

'Be sure to keep an eye on my husband,' she said. 'He ain't no horseman.'

'I will, ma'am,' Dale said. 'What's his name?'

'Will Doyle. You can't miss him. Headful of red hair.'

Dale doffed his hat once more. 'Be seein' you, ma'am,' he said.

'Good luck and good huntin', mister.'
He smiled and left the store.

On reaching the livery, he saw a group of eight men huddled by the livery door.

Al Croop noticed him at once and waved enthusiastically. 'Welcome, mister, the more guns the merrier.' Croop rushed to greet Dale, his hand outstretched.

'Name's Smith,' Dale said, 'Dale Smith.'

'I'm Al Croop and this here is Sheriff Clint West.'

Dale nodded. Then Croop introduced the rest of the posse. The names flew over Dale's head; he'd learn them one by one on the ride.

'Listen up, folks,' West began. 'We're gonna start by followin' the trail to Dewsburg. Klugg always stays over there when he's away on business, so I hope he did last night. After that, hell knows. Let's ride!'

Once mounted, West turned to Jack Jimson, who, West had decided, should stay in town and keep an eye on things.

'Keep your eyes and ears open, Jack. I'll get word to you whenever I can.'

'OK, Sheriff. Good luck.'

Jack watched as the posse walked their mounts out of the alleyway and turned left on Main, heading north-west, and thought, *You'll need it, Sheriff!*

Once out of town the eight riders, with West and Croop in the lead, began a slow canter. The ground was soft and slippery, and they didn't want to injure their mounts — or themselves.

The rain had stopped and visibility was getting better as the clouds began to burn away under the heat of the almost midday sun.

Pools of standing water were everywhere, but the men knew they'd quickly dry up.

The river, which ran north-east and was the reason Springfield was where it was, was still fast-flowing; the ford was deeper than West would have liked, but they had to cross it and there was no guarantee it would be any easier further north.

As they eased their mounts into the fast-flowing river, the water soon came up to stirrup level,

'Take it easy, men, single file and follow my path as we cross.'

One by one the men entered the river, careful to follow the sheriff's lead. The current was stronger than they had expected and the animals laid their ears back tight to their heads as the water rushed past their legs.

All went well until one of the horses panicked. It reared and, as it did so, the strength of the current forced the animal on to one side, throwing its rider, who seemed helpless to right the animal.

He tried to keep a hold of the reins, but as he landed in the water and went under, he lost his grip.

The man re-emerged some twenty feet downstream, where the water was much deeper and the current seemed to pick up pace.

The posse watched in both horror and helplessness as the man struggled.

The cowboy obviously couldn't swim. His head appeared twice above the water and the men waited for him to reappear.

But he never did.

'Goddamn!' yelled West. 'Who was that?'

'Think it was Will,' one of the riders said.

'He own the general store?' Dale asked.

'Well, he did,' came the reply.

'*Shee-it!* I jus' met his wife. She asked me to keep an eye on him.'

'Well, ain't your fault, fella. Be a sad loss to the town though.'

The remaining seven men reached the far bank and dismounted. Al turned his horse and walked it downstream aways, to see if he could find Will Doyle. But there was no sign of the man. Reluctantly, he turned his horse and returned to the group of men.

'No sign of him or his horse,' Croop

said as he dismounted.

'He'll be well downriver by now,' West said. 'That current sure is strong. I should never have let Will come along, he ain't no horseman.'

Silence ensued. To lose a friend so early in their quest had set them back a mite. It had turned what most of them had anticipated as a bit of excitement in their otherwise hundrum lives into what now they considered a dangerous and perilous journey.

Both West and Dale knew there was doubt creeping into the minds of the townsfolk. Most of them were middle-aged and had come along to get out of the way of their wives for a while. Now reality had set in and it wasn't quite the jaunt they'd expected.

'Any of you men wanna quit, now's the time to do it,' West said. 'Ain't no shame in it. What happened to Will coulda happened to any of us. This is a search party. All I wanna do is try and establish what happened to Seth Klugg and the whereabouts of the Parrys. We ain't looking for no gunplay, but if it turns out that the Parrys had anything to do with Klugg's disappearance and the death of Abe, well . . . '

He left the sentence hanging. He could see the men were concerned now, to do the right thing.

The men remained silent for a few moments before one of them spoke up.

Jake Williams ran the gunsmith's and doubled up as the undertaker; some joked that he supplied the means to an end.

'I think I speak for the rest of the men here, Sheriff. We go on.'

''Preciate that, men. Let's mount up and get this done.'

★   ★   ★

Clay woke with a start. He had no idea how long he'd slept; looking out of the window he saw that it was still daylight, and he gave a sigh of relief at that.

He got off the bed and put his

gunbelt on, walked to the window and looked down on Main Street. Plenty of folks were about and the rain had stopped; unbelievably, the morass of mud he'd had to walk through was drying up: the ground was still soft but not a cloying mess any more.

He splashed water on his face and reached for his Stetson. He unlocked the door and peered into the hallway to make sure Ma Dooley wasn't hovering anywhere near. It was clear. On an impulse, he decided he'd leave a marker. Quietly he closed the door and he looked around the room. The threadbare rug caught his attention; kneeling, he pulled off a single strand. Opening the door again, he held the strand near the top of the door, then closed it.

The material was barely noticeable as he locked the door — but he'd know if anyone had entered the room in his absence.

Making as little noise as possible, he went downstairs into the hallway. Just as he reached Ma Dooley's door it swung open.

'How's he doin'?' she asked.

'Just gone back to sleep,' Clay lied. 'A few more hours should see him right.'

'I'll hold off on that soup then,' she said.

'Good idea, I'll be back later an' see how he's doin'.'

Ma Dooley nodded and closed her door.

Not for one minute did Clay think she would let it go at that; he'd have to think on it later.

Casually, he strode down Main Street towards the bank, stopping now and then to look in a storefront and once to light a stogie.

Certain that no one was taking any notice of him, he turned into the alley that led to the rear of the bank.

After he'd knocked three times the door opened slightly until Wes could see who it was. Then he let Clay in.

'What ya find out?' Wes asked.

'Well, they found ol' Abe, and the sheriff organized a posse to go look for Klugg — and the Parrys.'

There was a sudden intake of breath from Lucy.

'When Klugg's horse turned up they sent a man to the Parry place to let Luther know, but of course, it was empty. Then they found Abe in the stables, put two and two together and came up with five.'

Wes grinned. 'You mean they think the Parrys are suspects?'

'Looks that way. Anyways, Dale signed up for the posse.'

'*What!*'

'Well, listen up. It makes sense. Dale figured that, folks knowing you were ill an' me still here in town, Dale volunteering would sure keep us in the clear.'

Wes was silent for a moment, then his grin returned.

'Hot dog!' he said. 'That *does* make sense.'

Inwardly, Clay breathed a sigh of

relief. He'd seen Wes lose his temper before and didn't want that experience again.

Luther and Lucy glanced at each other, both realizing that they could be held responsible and there wasn't a damn thing they could do about it.

'One problem, though,' Clay felt impelled to add. 'Ma Dooley's getting mighty nosy. She's made chicken soup for you.'

'Hmm,' Wes thought. 'Maybe I should make an appearance.'

'Would sure quieten her down,' Clay said.

'Could do with some chicken soup anyways.' Wes laughed. 'You be OK to stay here and keep an eye on these two while I'm gone? I'll be as quick as I can.'

'Sure, no problem.'

'Remember, three knocks is the signal,' Wes said as he went to leave the bank for the first time that day.

'Oh, Wes.' Clay caught his arm. 'I put me a small piece of cloth in the doorframe, in case Ma Dooley had a sneaky peak,

'Good thinkin', Clay.' Wes couldn't keep the surprise out of his voice.

7

The going was getting easier for the posse as the ground began to dry out. There were still huge pools of standing water and the wildlife was taking full advantage.

Signs of a flash flood were everywhere, the trail was littered with broken branches, tree stumps and rocks of all shapes and sizes, as well as dead animals.

Looking back, Clint West could see where the flood had run, an almost clear path led from the foothills about a mile distant.

Dale turned to see what the sheriff was looking at.

'Mother Nature sure is a powerful lady,' Dale muttered.

'Sure is,' West replied.

The posse were keeping their eyes glued to the stricken trail, looking for sign.

'Reckon the bank manager got caught in the flood, Sheriff?' Dale asked as he eased his mount round a large boulder.

'Mighta finished him off,' the sheriff replied, 'but there was blood on the saddle of his horse, so I reckon he was bushwhacked. Maybe they killed him, maybe he was jus' wounded. Either way, I ain't holdin' my breath on finding him alive; fact is, I don't reckon we'll even find him.'

'Bushwhacking seems the favourite,' Dale said. 'Otherwise the horse wouldn't have got back to town in one piece.'

'True enough,' the sheriff said. 'You're smarter than you look, mister.'

'I'll take that as a compliment, Sheriff!'

West grunted. 'Ten minutes, men,' he shouted.

A fire was quickly started and the coffee pot set in the flames; ten minutes was an awful short time but the men aimed to make the most of it.

Most of the men took a leak, then

gulped down the hot coffee as they smoked. Dale fished out his jerky and offered some to West.

West took it gratefully and both men chewed in silence. Until West said, 'Martha Doyle?'

'Yup,' Dale replied.

'There's a fork in the trail about half a mile ahead,' West said. 'It's a kind of short cut but a far rougher trail. Cuts about thirty minutes off the time to Dewsburg. Reckon we should split up there and meet where the trails join.'

'Makes sense,' Dale said.

'Thing is,' West went on, 'Al Croop is keen and eager enough, but I don't reckon on him taking charge when we split. He ain't got the experience.'

'Who you got in mind, Sheriff?' Dale asked.

'You. Reckon you can handle it?'

'Sure. You pick the men, OK?'

West stood up and addressed the posse; he told the men what was going to happen.

Al Croop looked a little miffed, but

West told him he needed him, which sort of appeased the young deputy.

They reached the fork some twenty minutes later. The short cut looked impassable from the main trail but it had to be checked out. West had no idea whether Klugg had used it or not.

The main trail seemed clearer here as the flash flood had followed a natural course downslope, bypassing the higher ground.

'OK, this is where we split up. Either group finds anything ya fire two shots, that'll signal the other group to join ya. Got that?'

The men nodded, there was no need for words.

'You men,' he turned to Dale's group, 'should get back on the main trail before we reach the fork, unless there's a hold-up somewhere along the line, so whoever gets there first waits.'

Dale led his two men, the barber, Cofa White, and Carl James, who ran a fancy-goods store, down the short cut carefully. There was more debris here

109

than on the main trail. The land sloped down into a small gully before rising up again slightly.

The vegetation damage was incredible and showed the power of the flash flood as it raced through, smashing and crushing everything in its path; it was almost unbelievable, the power the rushing water had as it carried boulders as well as tree trunks along with it.

The three men rode silently as they steered their horses along the rough trail; it would be all too easy for one of the animals to lose its footing and maybe take a fall or, worse still, break a leg.

They had been riding for thirty minutes before Dale raised a hand and pointed ahead. 'Dead horse,' he said,

Their mounts snorted as they caught the scent of the dead animal, but the riders kept them steady as they approached.

Dale dismounted and ground-hitched his horse. A few small clumps of grass were enough to distract his horse.

Reaching the dead animal, Dale pulled his bandanna up over his mouth and nose. The stench and the buzzing insects was grotesque, he could still smell death through his bandanna.

The animal was on its side, legs buckled up, two of the legs were clearly broken and the animal's belly was bloated.

Dale glanced upwards, but there were no buzzards circling. Maybe, he thought, they had other carcasses to feast on.

Dale gingerly inspected the animal. There was no brand visible. Bridle and reins were still attached and the saddle was a Western, so the unfortunate rider was maybe a cattleman.

He walked behind the animal, just to make sure there was no one buried beneath it.

It was clear.

'Must be a rider somewhere along the line,' Dale said. The other two men had joined him by now and they stared at the bloated animal.

'Don't suppose either of you recognize the horse?' Dale asked.

Both shook their heads. 'Nah, just a working line horse by the looks of it,' one of the men said.

'OK, let's mount up. Spread out a little and keep your eyes peeled.'

'You not gonna fire two shots?' Carl asked.

'For a dead horse?' Dale replied. 'We find a man, then we fire the shots.'

The three men mounted and spread out, walking their horses onwards.

* * *

Wes Brown made his way through the back alley, keeping off Main Street for as long as he could. He sure could use a beer, but decided to get back to Ma Dooley's first.

Make himself seen after he'd made sure his alibi had worked.

He reached the end of an alleyway

that was almost opposite the rooming-house. It seemed quiet enough. A few townsfolk were about, mostly brushing the splattered mud off the boardwalks.

West crossed the street and, on reaching the small veranda, took his boots off and opened the front door of Ma Dooley's place as quietly as he could.

Inside the hall all was quiet. Maybe Ma Dooley was having herslf a siesta, he thought.

Wes crept up the stairs and reached the door of their room.

The small piece of material was nowhere to be seen.

Damn! he thought and quickly entered the room locking the door behind him.

His brain raced as he began to think up a good reason why he hadn't been in the room.

Easy, he thought, *I just went out for some air. No need to elaborate.*

Wes decided to lie on the bed for a while and then go down to the saloon.

He took his gun-rig off and lay back, hands behind his head and stared at the ceiling.

He began to wonder about Dale.

They only had until 10.00 a.m. Monday morning, when the bank was due to open, to get the money from the safe, one way or another.

Whatever happened, the safe had to be cracked in the small hours of Monday morning.

The sheriff and a deputy were out of town so the chances of getting away were good. But what if Dale wasn't back?

If they left it might implicate him. No *might* about it, he thought. Maybe Dale could talk his way out of it, after all, he had volunteered for the posse, showing his eagerness to help.

But then there were the Parrys. They would be witnesses.

Wes reasoned his options: take them as hostages, bribe them with some of the loot, or — *kill them!*

Wes shuddered at the last option.

He'd never killed anyone in his life. So if push came to shove . . . ?

Wes sat up and decided he'd stayed long enough and no amount of thinking right now would do any good.

He put his gunbelt back on, and grabbed his Stetson.

He unlocked the door and stepped into the hallway just as Ma Dooley reached the top of the stairs.

'Well,' she said, 'you sure made a fast recovery!'

'Feelin' much better, thanks ma'am.'

'Didn't hear you go out,' she said accusingly.

'Didn't see you about either, ma'am. Had to get some fresh air.'

Ma Dooley stared at him awhile, then hummphed. 'Well, I got ya some chicken soup if'n ya can take it,' she said.

'Thank you kindly ma'am, but I had a bite while I was out, but would sure welcome it later.'

'Well, knock on my door when you return, in case I don't hear you again,' she added caustically.

Wes donned his Stetson, doffed it and left.

He really needed a drink now.

★   ★   ★

In the Golden Horn, Wilbur Enright was a worried man. What the hell had happened to Seth Klugg? Had he done a runner with the money? The title deeds to the land they'd bought were in the safe at the bank, and he had no way of getting at them.

The posse had been gone for nearly three hours now, and Enright rued the fact that he'd been asleep when they left, so was unable to have any of his men *volunteer*.

Maybe it wasn't too late. He called two of his henchmen over and instructed them to ride to Dewsburg. He needed information and he needed it fast.

'Make sure you're loaded,' he said. 'There might be some shootin' to do.'

Both men looked to one another. 'Who're we shootin' at?'

Enright went on to explain that he needed to find Klugg before the posse did and get the key to the safe. If they met any resistance, well, they'd know what to do. He added, 'I sure won't lose no sleep if'n the sheriff was to meet, say, an unfortunate accident. If you get my drift. There's a bonus in it for you of a hundred dollars, two hundred if you get the key.'

The two men left the saloon by the rear entrance, ran to the saloon's stable and readied their horses. Within ten minutes they headed out of town at a gallop.

Enright sat back and sipped his first whiskey of the day, certain that his two men could handle a bunch of store-keepers and a sheriff who was past it.

He smiled and lit a cigar just as Wes Brown pushed though the batwings.

Enright frowned as a thought hit him. He hadn't seen the three strangers around town at the same time. Just in twos and now one. What were they up to, he wondered.

'Care to join me for a drink?' he called to Wes. 'Marty, bring a bottle over and a glass for my friend here. The good stuff, mind.'

'Sure thing, boss,' the 'keep replied.

Wes removed his Stetson and sauntered across to Enright.

'Don't believe we've formally met,' Enright said. 'I'm Wilbur Enright, owner of this establishment, and you are . . . ?'

'Wes Brown.' Wes sat down at the table.

The 'keep arrived and placed a shot glass in front of Wes, refilled Enright's glass and then filled Wes's.

'So, Mr Brown, what brings you to our fair town?' Enright asked.

'Jus' passin' through, Mr Enright. Me and my pards are on our way West, California maybe. Needed to rest up awhile as I fell ill. Something I ate on the trail, I think.'

Wes picked up his glass, held it

towards Enright, and said, 'Good health and thanks, Mr Enright, mighty fine whiskey.'

'Yours, too, Mr Brown. Yours too.'

★   ★   ★

Clay was getting edgy.

It was nearly two hours since Wes had left and the silence in the bank was getting to him.

He glanced across at the Parrys. Lucy was sleeping, her head lolling to one side. Luther was wide awake and Clay felt his eyes boring into him.

For the umpteenth time, Clay walked across to the huge safe and stood looking at it.

Inside that great hunk of metal sat the answer to all Clay's dreams. Riches beyond imagination. He fiddled with the combination, spinning it left and right, a vague hope that by some miracle he'd find the right combination.

But he knew that even if he did, he'd still need the key.

He kicked the safe viciously with his left boot, and then cursed as the pain shot up his leg.

'Goddamn!' he yelled.

The sudden noise woke Lucy with a start. Luther looked across at her and winked, smiling beneath his gag.

Both were parched. It seemed as if the gag was sucking the moisture from their bodies.

Clay sat, nursing his foot and cursing the bank manager for not being there.

Outside, Clay could hear the usual noises of a small town. The clunk of boots on the boardwalk, a horse whinnying, the sounds of children laughing: normality, he thought.

He picked up the saddle-bag and opened the flap to look at the money inside. He pulled out a wad and flicked through it; it almost made his mouth water.

Maybe they should cut their losses and just leave? Quit while they were ahead.

A sudden wave of tiredness swept

through Clay. He put the saddle-bag down and walked across to the large desk that dominated the office. Behind it sat the manager's chair. Clay settled in it, put his feet up on the desk, took a look at the Parrys, knowing, but making sure, they were secure; took a deep breath and closed his eyes.

* * *

Dale again led the way down the trail, which became noticably more difficult to negotiate. Rocks and boulders were strewn everywhere along with cactus, cottonwoods and joshuas, all ripped up by the roots to form a landscape that looked like a scene from hell.

Amongst the debris small animals, horribly crushed, some stripped of their fur completely, lay in contorted positions.

The smell was getting stronger. The sun's cruel rays, reflected from the parched land, set up a shimmering heat-haze of death and destruction which filled their eyesight.

All three had their bandannas tightly wrapped around their faces, but they did little to prevent the stench from turning their stomachs.

They halted their animals abruptly. All three saw the same sickening sight at the same time.

The semi-naked body lay on its back. The eyes had been pecked out and the arms were half-raised, hands clawed as if to fight off certain death.

Flesh had been stripped from the upper half of the body, muscle and sinew clearly visible through the haze of flies feasting on the remains.

Overhead, buzzards circled, clearly waiting their chance at a meal.

Cofa White was the first man to spill his guts, Carl gagged and it took Dale a great deal of effort not to follow suit.

Dale dismounted on legs that felt like jelly as he approached the gruesome sight.

The lower half of the body was still clothed, except for one boot missing revealing a foot that was unrecognizable.

Carl and Cofa dismounted, wiping their faces and all three men took their Stetsons off.

But who was this man?

8

Ben Ramirez and Nat Baker reined in their mounts as soon as they heard the two gunshots.

Turning their heads every whichway they tried to ascertain the direction of the shots.

It was impossible, except to say it was somewhere ahead.

'What ya reckon?' Nat asked.

'Could be trouble, or could be someone in trouble,' Ben replied.

They waited for a few minutes in case any more shots were fired, but there were none. Apart from a gentle breeze rustling the now dried-out vegetation, there was silence.

Both men spurred their mounts forward at a steady canter; whatever those two shots meant, they knew the posse wasn't far ahead.

They reined to a halt at the junction

of the two trails. Ben dismounted and looked for sign.

'Seems they split here,' he said. 'Three horses took the short cut, four stayed on the main trail.'

'Makes sense,' Nat replied. 'I got a hankering to use the short cut. What say you?'

Ben stood and casually took out his makings. He expertly rolled a stogie and lit it, inhaling deeply.

His steel-grey eyes surveyed the terrain.

'Land slopes off to the right,' he said. 'Flood's followed that. Anyone caught out here would be swept down there.' He pointed to the short cut.

'That's what I was thinkin',' Nat said. 'If Klugg got this far, he'll be down there someplace.'

Ben finished his cigarette and threw the butt to the ground. 'Well, let's see how good this posse is.' He remounted and they steered their horses down the slope.

★　★　★

West raised a hand and called a halt. The two shots echoed slightly. He took out his field glasses and swept his line of vision downslope towards the short cut trail.

They were no more than an hour tops from Dewsburg, and from their vantage point some 200 feet above the short cut, he was hoping he'd see some sign of movement.

There was none.

The downslope was littered with vegetation and a line of trees obscured any view he might have had of the trail.

'Reckon the junction is about a mile yonder,' he said, looking down the trail. 'Let's get going.'

The main trail was relatively clear. The storm and heavy rain had caused a few mud slides but the ground itself was mainly clear, making their progress much easier.

They set off at a gentle gallop, reaching the junction in under five minutes.

West veered off the main trail and led

the men down the gentle slope.

Again, the trail here, although rougher than the main trail, was mostly clear of storm damage. It was little used, even though it cut the journey time between Dewsburg and Springfield by anything up to forty-five minutes, as the trail was too rough and there was a danger of crippling a horse.

The posse slowed to a walk, picking their way through the rocks and stones that littered the trail.

They passed by a clump of Joshua trees whose stumpy branches offered some shelter from both sun and rain and West called a halt.

He dismounted and, kneeling, took out a bandanna and dried the inner rim of his Stetson and the back of his neck.

'Sign here, boys,' he said. 'Two horses; the tracks aren't clear but they ain't that old.'

'You reckon Klugg came this way, Sheriff?' one of the men asked.

'Don't reckon Klugg was that good a

horseman,' the sheriff offered. 'He was more used to sitting at a desk than sitting a pony.'

The man grinned. 'Ain't that a fact,' he said.

'No,' the sheriff went on. 'Whoever made these tracks it weren't Klugg.'

The sheriff stood, placed his Stetson on his head and took down his canteen. Taking out the stopper, he took a mouthful.

He mounted up. 'Come on,' he said. 'Let's go see what Dale's found.'

* * *

'That sure ain't Klugg,' Cofa White said.

'How'd ya know?' Dale asked.

'Klugg's a big man — and fat! That critter is as skinny as a fence-post.'

Dale pondered this.

Grimacing beneath his bandanna, Dale knelt by the body — what there was of it.

'I'll check his pants pockets, see if

there's anything on him.'

He rose up to his feet, walked to his mount and retrieved a pair of leather gloves. No way was he putting his bare hands near that body.

It was fruitless, however as both side pockets were empty.

'Give me a hand here,' Dale said. 'I gotta check his back pockets.'

Reluctantly, Carl approached the body, and between them they rolled it onto its side.

'What the — '

Both men stood and stepped back. The man's back was sliced open. A huge gash ran diagonally from his left shoulder, exposing the spine and down almost to his hips.

As they watched, gagging, a steaming pile of guts slid out and spread over the ground.

The stench was indescribable.

Dale reeled, and threw up beneath his bandanna, Carl and Cofa stepped back quickly, trying to get the vile stench from their nostrils.

Dale ripped off his bandanna and wiped his mouth.

'Sorry about that,' he apologized.

'All we could do not to follow suit,' Cofa replied. 'I ain't never seen nothin' like that!'

'Better get it covered,' Dale said. 'Grab a tarp and we'll pin it down with some rocks, there's plenty to choose from.'

As he began to cover the body, Dale stopped.

'Well, I'll be a — '

'What is it?' Carl asked.

'This fella's been shot! Look at his neck for chris'sake, damn near took his head off.'

'I'll take your word for it, Dale,' Carl replied.

'Me too,' Cofa added. 'Seen more'n enough already.'

Dale hauled the tarp over the body and made it as secure as they could, then they mounted up.

'Well, if that ain't Klugg, maybe he's further along the trail,' Dale said.

'We'll soon find out, I guess,' Cofa said, not hiding his fear of the discovery. He'd done a bit of sawbones work in his time, some bloody, but never anything as gruesome as the body he'd just seen.

'Let's ride,' Dale said. 'No sense hangin' around here.'

★   ★   ★

Jack Jimson watched as the good folks of Springfield left the small church on the outskirts of town.

Hypocrites! he thought. The menfolk will probably head straight for the saloon, while their wives take the children home and start the Sunday dinner.

Jack had ambitions. Those ambitions were to be the sheriff of Springfield.

He walked back to the sheriff's office, his mind in a whirl. For weeks now, he'd been keeping a secret eye on Klugg and Enright, as well as on Clint West. But he couldn't find any evidence

— yet — that would stand up in a court of law.

The landgrabbing — or repossession, as Klugg called it — seemed to be above-board.

But Jimson had followed Klugg many times, late at night, to the saloon where he and Enright had retired to the saloon owner's office.

West always arrived later on.

They were connected, his gut told him, all he needed was proof.

Maybe that proof was in the safe?

Jimson set the coffee pot on the stove and sank into the sheriff's chair. His brain was whirring. There had to be something he'd missed. But for the life of him he couldn't figure out what.

He'd been through the sheriff's desk — even the locked bottom drawer — but found nothing.

He'd searched the sheriff's room at the side of the office — again nothing.

Jimson didn't believe West was that clever. He was just their lackey, there to do their bidding.

He'd drawn a blank and found nothing.

But he would.

Or die in the attempt.

★   ★   ★

Enright was becoming increasingly concerned. Maybe he should have gone with his henchmen, but then, he had West in his pocket, and the two men he'd sent after the posse were seasoned gunnies. He'd seen them in action many times in the saloon. Gunplay was frequent when men thought they'd been cheated out of their hard-earned wages.

And cheated they were.

Enright was a master of his craft and when trouble flared, Ramirez and Baker took care of it.

Death was the inevitable outcome of the unsuspecting rannie who was aggrieved.

Suddenly, Enright smiled. Yes, he thought, they'd take care of things.

* * *

Wes finished his tour of the town, making sure as many people as possible saw him.

He tipped his hat at every woman he came across, showing a beaming smile and saying, 'Afternoon, ma'am.' He knew they'd remember that.

Now it was time to get back to Clay.

Ducking down an alleyway, he headed towards the rear of the bank.

As usual the alleyways were empty. Wes imagined that during a working day they would be busy but today being Sunday . . .

He was still cautious. He halted at the corner of the alley that passed the rear of the bank and peered round. Again, empty, so Wes quickly made his way to the door and knocked three times.

He waited.

'Goddamn, Clay!' he muttered under his breath.

He knocked three times again.

This time the door eased open, Clay's sleep-filled face poked out and Wes slipped inside. Quickly he closed the door.

'Took your sweet time,' Wes said.

'Sorry, was half-asleep. Kinda boring jus' sittin' here all day.'

Wes looked across the room to the Parrys, who were still tightly bound and gagged; and he breathed a sigh of relief.

'Boring or not, we got a job to do so let's do it. If Dale ain't back come midnight, we blow the safe and get outa here. I ain't waitin' longer than that.'

'Suits me fine,' Clay responded. 'I hate being cooped up like a chicken.'

The clock showed 4.10. *Less than eight hours to wait!*

*   *   *

Dale and his men had ridden no more than a hundred yards when they came upon another horse.

This one was alive though. It lay about ten feet up a small slope, and

135

immediately Dale saw the animal's rear right leg was severely damaged. Dismounting, he slowly approached the animal, careful not to panic it any more than it already was.

The horse's eyes were wide, showing white and the ears pinned back as Dale knelt beside it.

He spoke softly as he gently stroked the animal's rump. 'Whoa, boy, let's take a look at that leg.'

He turned to Cofa and Carl and shook his head. 'Leg's bust, more'n once by the look of it. Only thing we can do is put him out of his misery.'

Carl and Cofa looked at one another. Dale could see that neither of them was willing to ease the poor animal's plight. The most they had killed between them was swatting flies.

'I'll do it,' Dale said. 'You boys can turn away, it's OK.'

Both gladly did so.

Dale stood, took out his revolver and walked to the front of the horse.

He knelt down and stroked the

horse's neck, whispering: 'Good boy, good boy,' and the horse snickered.

His ears were upright and the panic in his eyes vanished. Dale thought, *it seems to know.*

He cocked the Colt and squeezed the trigger.

The horse shuddered once as the bullet entered its brain, then lay still.

Dale stood, the smoking handgun at his side. He quickly wiped a tear from his eye as Carl and Cofa turned round to face him.

'You did the right thing, Dale,' Cofa said. Carl nodded.

'Yeah. I know. But it sure don't make me feel better none.' He slid the revolver back in its holster and walked to his own horse.

He mounted up, as did Carl and Cofa, and they set off down the trail, fearful of what other horrors awaited them.

★   ★   ★

Ramirez and Baker reined in. The shot was much closer than the first two and they got a fix on it.

'No more'n half a mile,' Ramirez said. 'Look, fresh tracks, but only three horses as far as I can see.' He pointed to a clear patch of dirt and sand that wasn't littered with debris.

'Thought there was eight,' Baker said.

'There was,' Ramirez said, adding, 'They split up at the junction, remember?'

'Don't make no sense splitting five to three,' Baker said.

'Maybe somethin' happened,' Ramirez pointed out.

'You mean those two shots?'

'No, I doubt it. We'da found a body or at least some sign.'

'The river!' Baker said. 'Musta been there; these townsmen ain't no horsemen.'

'Amen to that,' Ramirez said.

'Let's go find out what's goin' on,' Baker said. 'Those greenhorns ain't that savvy out here.' They moved down.

* ★ ★

At the same time, Sheriff Clint West halted the posse and waited for the second shot. But it never came.

'What the hell!' he exclaimed.

Jake Williams pulled up alongside the sheriff. 'What ya reckon, Clint?'

'Don't know but I don't like it an' that's for sure.' He turned to the other men. 'Keep your eyes peeled, men, and your guns ready.'

He waved a hand and they moved on.

There was a tense atmosphere now as the men realized this was no Sunday jaunt.

Something was going on down here and they were being drawn into it.

And that they did not like. West had said it was going to be a 'search party'. They'd already lost a friend; now they began to fear for their own safety.

West could feel the change in atmosphere as they slowly proceeded down the trail.

9

They came across Klugg's body ten minutes later, or rather, they came across the buzzards feasting on a body.

'Don't think I can take much more of this,' Dale said as they dismounted.

The buzzards reluctantly departed, soon to be circling overhead waiting to get back down again.

There was less of a smell here, presumably because Klugg's innards had already been devoured.

Cofa and Carl stood by Dale as they looked at the mutilated body.

Like the other corpse, all he had on was his pants, his boots had managed to stay put, and again the body was flat on its back.

What was different was two things: half the head was missing and the stomach was wide open.

'Jeez!' Cofa said. 'What a mess.'

The buzz of flies started up as they saw their opportunity to feed now the buzzards had left.

Dale removed his hat and swatted them away as best he could, but the insects were resilient and weren't to be put off that easily.

'Either of you recognize him?' Dale asked.

'Yeah, that's Klugg all right. See that ring on his pinky there,' Cofa said, 'seen that many times when trimming his hair and giving him that there banker shave. It's Klugg all right.'

Carl nodded in agreement,

'Weren't the flood that finished him off,' Dale said. 'A slug took the top of his head off. This man's been bush-whacked.'

'I'll be danged,' Cofa said. 'Still, ain't surprised, the man was despised.'

'How so?' Dale asked.

'Well . . .' Cofa hesitated. 'Not that there's any proof, but a lot of folks reckon as to how he ran the home-steaders off'n their land. All seems above-board, but, well, you know folks.'

'Any one in particular?' Dale asked.

'Could be one of many. Hell, he expected me to barber him for free.'

'And did you?' Dale had a grin on his face.

'Hell no, I own my building, weren't beholden to him fer anything!' Cofa seemed quite indignant.

Dale returned his gaze to the body. 'Well, we got ourselves a killin', that's for sure.'

'You think maybe that critter back yonder had anything to do with it?'

'Could be, who knows? But I doubt it,' Dale said. 'Unless they both shot each other at the same time. Maybe when the sheriff gets here he'll recognize what's left of the man.'

They were so engrossed in Klugg's body that they failed to hear the approaching horsemen.

Dale turned sharply, expecting to see the sheriff and his men. Instead he saw two mean-looking *hombres*, whose lips smiled but their eyes didn't.

142

Both Carl and Cofa recognized them immediately.

'They're Enright's men,' Cofa whispered to Dale.

Dale called out a 'howdy', the two men didn't respond.

'What brings you gents out here?' Dale asked.

Ramirez shifted in his saddle, revealing a pearl-handled revolver.

'On an errand for Mr Enright,' he said.

'What you got there?' Baker asked.

'Seth Klugg, or rather what's left of him. Had the top of his head shot off,' Dale replied.

Baker looked at Ramirez.

'He got anything on him?' Ramirez asked.

'Not a plug nickel,' Dale answered and suspicion formed in his mind. *What sort of a question was that?*

'You wouldn't be holdin' out on us, would you, mister?' Ramirez asked, and Dale saw his right hand leave the reins and slowly lower towards his holster.

Carl and Cofa had slowly edged back a tad as Dale answered.

'Holdin' out on what, exactly?'

'You tryin' to be smart with us, mister?' Baker's voice had an edge to it that Dale didn't care for.

'Mister, whoever you are, we're deputized and came out here to find out what happened to Klugg. We found out what, but we ain't found out why and who.'

'I'll ask you one more time, mister,' Ramirez threatened. 'You find anything on Klugg's body?'

'An' I'll tell you one more time, we ain't found a thing. Look for yourself.'

Ramirez drew, Dale had expected it and although Ramirez was fast, Dale was faster.

Before Ramirez's gun was clear of the holster, Dale had drawn and his Colt was pointing at the man. At this range he couldn't miss.

Ramirez let his revolver slide back into its holster.

'This ain't over, mister,' Ramirez snarled.

'Oh I think me an' Mr Colt here think it is. I was you I'd ride on and finish your errand. I won't be so generous next time.'

'Come on, let's get out of here, Ben,' Baker urged.

Ramirez fixed Dale with a stare that would split rock, but he dug his spurs viciously into his mount and set off in the direction of Dewsburg. Baker followed but with less speed.

Dale watched them go, then holstered his gun.

'Jeez!' Carl said. 'You know who those two were?'

'Nope, and can't say I care much,' Dale said.

'They're only Enright's henchmen; they've killed more men than — well more than I can count.'

'Shootin' drunks in a saloon is child's play, any damn fool can do that,' Dale said.

'Oh, word has it they done more'n that in their time,' Cofa put his two cents in.

'They don't scare me none,' Dale said, and dismissed the subject.

'Let's get Klugg covered. Carl, fire off two shots will ya, let the sheriff know we found something else.'

Dale retrieved a tarp from his horse and started to cover the dead man, again piling rocks around it to keep it secure.

Carl duly fired two shots.

★   ★   ★

Ramirez reined in.

'That's it,' he said.

'What's it?' Baker asked.

'The two shots. They were a signal. Which means West took some of the posse along the main trail. I figure they're on their way down here right now, heading in from the Dewsburg end.'

The penny dropped with Baker. 'Be like a turkey shoot,' he enthused.

'Let's get to the higher ground and wait, they sure won't be long,' Ramirez said. He led his mount up a steep slope.

They reached a good vantage point and, after hitching the horses behind a clump of trees, they took their rifles and settled down to wait for the unsuspecting posse.

They didn't have to wait long.

Ramirez nudged Baker and pointed. 'West is in the lead,' he whispered.

Baker nodded.

'I'll take him, you take that fella at the back, that'll panic the other two and we can get them at our leisure,' Ramirez said with a sickly grin.

As Ramirez sighted down the barrel of his Winchester, he gently squeezed the trigger.

At that exact moment, Al Croop drew alongside West. He took the full impact of the .45 slug.

It looked to Ramirez as if his head had exploded in a fountain of blood.

Baker fired a split second later, downing the last man in the group of four riders.

The two remaining members of the

posse, West and Jake Williams, sat stock still for longer than they should have.

Shock filled their faces as they turned their mounts anxiously, hoping to get away.

For two expert gunnies, their escape was doomed.

Baker got Williams square in the back. The force of the slug threw him forward, his head landing on the horse's neck; as the animal reared and started a mad gallop, Williams's body was thrown to the ground.

If the shot hadn't killed him, landing head first on a jagged boulder certainly did.

Ramirez had waited, he enjoyed the unfair hunt, and wanted his prey to think he'd got away.

West stood no chance of that.

Taking careful aim, Ramirez once again squeezed the trigger. The slug caught West in the back of the neck. His mount, panicked by the sound of the shots and the smell of blood in its nostrils, fell as its hoofs caught a rock and sent it tumbling to the ground.

West was thrown to one side but, as the animal got back to his feet, West's right boot was trapped in the stirrup.

The animal galloped as fast as its legs would carry it, West's body bouncing from rock to rock.

Pretty soon he was a pulped mass of blood and gore — barely recognizable as a human being.

Baker and Ramirez stood up watching for any signs of movement from the other three bodies.

Of course, there was none. Neither man had expected there to be.

'Now we wait for the other three,' Ramirez said. 'The gunfire will have alerted them.'

Both men reloaded and lay down to wait.

★　★　★

Dale froze.

One, two, a pause, three, an even longer pause, four!

'I counted four shots!' The other men nodded.

'Goddamn! It must have been those two gunnies, thing is, who shot at who?'

'I got a pretty good idea,' Carl said.

'Me too,' Dale said.

'We better go take a looksee,' Cofa said, even though it was the last thing he wanted to do.

'Hold up there, Cofa. We might be riding into a trap. Those two fellas could be lyin' in wait for us. I sure don't wanna go down there and become sittin' ducks.' Dale paused.

'What do you propose?' Cofa asked.

'What would you do in that situation?' Dale asked.

Cofa thought for a minute or two before answering, 'Get to the high ground, I guess.'

'Exactly, an' that's what we're gonna do. I reckon those two fellas did that and just waited for West and the rest to ride on in. Picked 'em off one by one. Check your handguns and rifles, and keep those rifles out!' Dale checked his guns and mounted up.

'Silence from here on in,' Dale said. 'The ground up yonder is steep, but mostly sand-covered, so try and avoid any rocks. In this place the sound of metal hitting stone can be heard from a long way off.'

They set off, Indian-style, up the steepest part of the slope, meandering to find the best route.

After a steady climb, Dale raised a hand to call a halt and took out his field glasses.

Scanning the trail below, he slowly worked his way up the slopes ahead. All seemed quiet, he could see no movement but, just as he was about to put the glasses down, he caught sight of a horse.

Steadying his mount, he focused on the animal. It was hitched behind a clump of trees. Moving his field of vision slightly lower he finally saw what he was looking for.

Barely visible, he saw a black hat.

'Got 'em,' he said quietly.

Carl pulled up alongside him and whispered, 'You see 'em? Is it the sheriff? Or those two evil bastards Ramirez and Baker?'

'It ain't the sheriff,' Dale said in a low voice.

After fixing their position in his head, Dale scanned higher up, looking for the best line of attack.

Dale dismounted and beckoned the other two men to do the same.

Huddled, Dale went on to tell them his plan.

★   ★   ★

The clock in the bank manager's office showed 5.30. To Clay, who was becoming a little stir-crazy, every minute seemed to take an hour.

Wes looked at the agitated man seated before him. Noted his left leg tapping up and down rapidly as his nerves began to get the better of him.

'Stop clock-watching, Clay,' he said. 'We're safe in here, no one else has a key and it's Sunday, so no one expects the bank to be open and no one, no one suspects anything.'

'I know, Wes, it's just this waiting around. What if Dale don't get back here?'

'I told you, we blow the safe an' get out of here. Dale will have to make his own plans. The bank opens at ten tomorrow, if'n it don't . . . ' He didn't finish the sentence.

★ ★ ★

Jack Jimson sat in the sheriff's office drinking coffee. His mind was racing. Something was going down, he knew that, but what?

Nothing seemed to make any sense. The Parrys concerned him. He'd known Luther and Lucy for a few years now: Luther, a mild-mannered man in his early twenties, was a popular member of town, he couldn't think of anyone who didn't like him.

Then there was Lucy.

She was the sweetest, prettiest woman Jimson had ever known. Long auburn hair framed a face of beauty that set most men's hearts racing.

They were a devoted couple. Loved and, in some cases, envied by most of Springfield's townsfolk.

Did they disappear, or were they taken? If they'd done a runner, it would only be because of the money in the bank. But Jimson knew for a fact, the only person who had access to the safe was Klugg.

And Klugg had disappeared too.

If the Parrys were taken, it meant there was another party involved. But what if Klugg had robbed the bank?

And then there was Enright! Why had he sent two of his toughest henchmen out to look for Klugg? What could he hope to achieve by that?

Jimson had had a hunch for a long time that Enright and Klugg were in cahoots, and he was certain the sheriff was involved in some way.

But what if Klugg and Parry were in

it together? Where did that leave Enright?

The more Jimson thought about it, the more combinations seemed to appear, all of which made some kind of sense, yet the more befuddled he became.

He pulled open the bottom drawer of West's desk, pulled out a bottle of bourbon and a glass, and decided that what he needed most right now was a drink

* * *

Enright, for his part, was pacing his office. He continually took his hunter out to check the time, and continually topped his shot glass up. Not for him the crude rot-gut slops he sold over the counter. His was imported whisky from Scotland, and he savoured every mouthful.

Where the hell is Klugg? he thought for the umpteenth time that day.

He couldn't have done a runner, not

with the biggest land deal ever about to happen.

News of the railroad was still top secret, even the mayor didn't know. Just him and Klugg. And Klugg couldn't do the deal alone as the deeds had both names on them, so Enright's signature was essential for any transaction.

He'd made sure of that at the land registry office in Dewsburg.

He downed the whisky and poured another.

He sank into his plush leather chair set behind his Italian-styled desk, opened his French humidor and extracted a Cuban cigar.

He lovingly held it to his ear and rolled it between thumb and forefinger. Then ran it under his nose, inhaling the delicious aroma, almost making his mouth water.

He placed the cigar into the small French guillotine and neatly sliced the end off, then reached for a vesta. He held the flame near the cigar and puffed until he was satisfied it was well lit.

After extinguishing the vesta, he leaned back in his chair, cigar in his right hand, whisky in his left hand.

It couldn't get any better than this, he thought.

10

Ramirez was getting fidgety.

'They shoulda been here by now,' he said to Baker.

'Maybe they're being a tad circumspect,' Baker replied.

'What? What the hell does that mean?' Ramirez grated.

'You know, a bit wary.'

'Say what you mean then, don't go throwing no fancy words at me, I ain't in the mood.'

'OK, OK, calm down. They'll be here, just keep your cool and your eyes peeled.'

'You keep an eye on the trail, I'm gonna take a looksee up yonder. Don't want no backshooting from up there.'

'OK, keep low,' Baker advised.

Ramirez turned to say something, but changed his mind.

He belly-crawled up from their

position, to where the horses were hitched.

His own animal whinnied and snorted as it recognized its owner, the sound seemed deafening in the silence.

Ramirez stood, shielded by a tree trunk and peered from behind it, looking for any sign of movement.

He waited a few more moments, all was quiet.

Maybe, he thought, he was being over-cautious, but then, being cautious was what kept him alive. He took a last look around to make sure and then decided he'd given the townies too much credit.

He crouched low, and began to make his way back to Baker.

The shot that rang out took him completely by surprise, as did the pain in his right arm.

He fell flat on the ground on his belly and waited for more shots, but none came.

Rolling onto his back, he inspected his arm. Blood seeped through his shirtsleeve and he pulled it up to inspect the wound.

The slug had taken a chunk out of his forearm, but was only a flesh wound. He took off his bandanna, wound it tightly over the wound and lay back waiting for his mind to conquer the pain.

Fingers tingling, he started back towards Baker.

★   ★   ★

'Ya get him, Dale?' Cofa asked.

'Not sure,' Dale replied. 'I think I saw him go down, but . . . '

He picked up the field glasses and scanned the area. Tall grass and shrubs made a good hiding place and Dale saw no sign of his target. He lowered the glasses. 'Can't see any movement, but it's not worth taking any chances.'

'Agreed,' Carl said. 'So what do we do now?'

'Secure the horses, we go on foot from here on in,' Dale said. There was a steely edge to his voice now; it was becoming personal.

For the first time in his life he was respected as a man, given responsibility by a sheriff, and he wasn't about to let anyone down.

As if to reaffirm his thoughts, Cofa leaned across and said: 'Sure am glad we got you with us, Dale.'

Dale gave an embarrassed grin. 'Well, let's hope we all get out of this in one piece.'

'Amen to that,' Carl added.

'OK, let's go,' Dale said, 'and spread out, we don't want to make an easy target. Carl, you take the middle station, Cofa, slightly lower, I'll go up further. Keep sight of each other and for Pete's sake, keep your heads down.'

Moving slowly and silently, the trio made their way further north, Cofa and Carl keeping their eyes alternately on where they'd seen their quarry and Dale.

A shot rang out.

All three ducked down, but Carl was

a tad slower. The slug caught him on the shoulder, nicking it painfully, but not seriously. It would hamper his usefulness with a rifle though.

His grunt of pain was audible and Dale called out, 'Anyone hit?'

'Dagblast it!' Carl replied. 'Got a nick on the shoulder. Flesh wound but sure as all hell hurts some.'

'Cofa, you OK?'

'Yeah, I'm good.'

'Stay where you are, I'll go see Carl,' Dale told him.

Dale slid down the slope until he reached Carl's side.

'Let's take a looksee,' Dale said. He took out his knife, sliced open Carl's shirt at the elbow and slit upwards. There was plenty of blood, but Dale could see the bullet had winged Carl.

'Looks like you got a chipped collar bone, ol' buddy. Bullet passed right across.'

He took out a neckerchief from his back pocket, ripped Carl's shirtsleeve to make a pad, and tied the neckerchief over the shoulder, securing it under the armpit.

'That should stop the bleeding. We'll get the sawbones to stitch you up when we get back to town. You best stay put now, but keep that rifle handy, OK?'

'Sure, Dale,' Carl replied. 'Damn sorry I got hit.'

'Don't worry, we'll get you back soon.'

Dale climbed back up to his position and he and Carl edged forward.

* * *

Ramirez made it back to Baker more or less in one piece.

'You OK?' Baker asked.

'Got hit in the arm, but I think I got one of them. They're coming across the high land behind us.'

'I'll get the horses,' Baker said, 'no sense in us being sitting ducks.'

'I ain't runnin' out.' Ramirez almost spat the words out. 'That sonuverbitch made a fool of me an' he ain't gonna get away with it.'

'It ain't runnin' out, Ben. It's more a strategic withdrawal,' Nat Baker replied.

'You can call it any fancy name you like, it's still runnin' away,' Ramirez said in a raised voice.

'Keep your voice down,' Ben whispered.

Ramirez glared at Baker.

'Ben, you need a sawbones to take a look at that arm. How you gonna handle a six-gun? Answer me that.'

Ramirez was silent for a while. He was trying to flex his fingers. The tingling sensation was worse now and he had little control of his hand.

'Guess you're right,' Ramirez conceded.

'I'll get the horses, you keep low, we'll get back to town and report to the boss, OK?'

'OK.'

Ramirez hated defeat, but he knew that what Baker said was true. He needed to get his arm seen to, and pretty damn quick.

Baker had moved up the slope and neared the horses who were contentedly grazing on the sparse vegetation.

Reaching the clump of trees, he stood up and grabbed the reins of both animals. Using them as a shield, he led them down the slope and back to Ramirez.

'I need to fix your arm up,' Baker said.

He took off his bandanna and used it as a makeshift sling.

'That feel any better?' he asked.

'Sure, eased it a tad,' Ramirez grudgingly replied.

'Keep the horse in front of you,' Baker said, 'don't give them a clear shot at you.'

Ramirez nodded silently and the two descended to the trail.

★　★　★

'They're making a break for it,' Dale said. He peered through his field glasses. 'Using the horses as a shield.'

Dale followed their progress as the two men reached the trail again.

'What we gonna do?' Cofa asked.

'Wait up, I wanna see which way they go.'

It took them five minutes to reach the trail and, as Dale watched, they mounted up and turned north — heading towards Dewsburg.

'Right,' Dale said. He lowered the field glasses and turned to Cofa.

'They're heading towards Dewsburg, I reckon we go back to Carl and get him back to town. Once the doc's taken a look at him, I'll go and see the deputy, what's his name?'

'Jimson, Jack Jimson.'

'Right, Jimson, and tell him what's been going on.'

They made their way back to Carl. 'How you feeling, Carl?' Cofa asked, bending down to help the man to his feet.

'We're heading back to Springfield, get that wound seen to,' Dale said.

They helped him mount up and Dale

led the way back to the trail.

'If we ride steady,' Dale said as they took the trail back to Springfield, 'shouldn't take more'n two hours to get back.'

They passed the still-covered body of Klugg, then the mystery man and finally the horse. The trail was a gentle slope upwards now and they knew they'd soon reach the main trail, where the going would be easier.

*   *   *

Baker and Ramirez had reached the main trail as well; they'd headed north in order to avoid being shot at, now they turned left, heading south again along the trail. It would put them between forty minutes and an hour behind what was left of the posse.

Ramirez was in a lot of pain, but he spurred his animal on. He was filled with an almost uncontrollable hatred and his rage was building up with every yard they covered.

'Slow down, pard,' Baker said, riding alongside Ramirez. 'We got at least a two-hour ride an' we need to take care of the horses.'

Again, Ramirez knew Baker was right. He slowed down, both men now doing a steady canter and covering the ground well, but still not well enough for Ramirez.

His mind was on one thing, and one thing only.

To get even.

★　★　★

Wes Brown was asleep.

He was sitting in the manager's chair with his feet up on the desk as if he didn't have a care in the world.

The same could not be said of Clay Leghorn.

He'd sat for a while, fidgeted, stood up and wandered into the main bank area. He paced the area behind the counter, then walked to the front doors. He was tempted to take a peek at the side of the blinds, but resisted.

Knowing his luck, someone would see him.

It was now 8.15.

Where the hell was Dale? he wondered.

Clay walked to the counter and undid the saddle-bags. Inside were eight sticks of dynamite and a length of fuse wire.

He took the eight sticks out and placed them side by side on the counter.

Next he took out a ball of string. Making two bundles of four, he tied the sticks together.

There was eighteen inches of fuse wire, which he cut in half. He wouldn't insert the fuses yet, but nine inches was long enough for them all to get clear before they blasted the safe.

With only a rudimentary knowledge of dynamite, neither Clay nor Wes knew whether the charge would be enough or too much.

Their only experience was watching

as rocks were blown from a hillside to be used to make a dam.

There was two feet of fuse on those sticks, he recalled, and it seemed to take an age for them to burn down.

Unseen, Clay had helped himself to the sticks stored in a shed near the dam site.

He'd done it on a whim, with no particular reason in mind, but thought it could be useful sometime.

Little did he know that it had sown the seed of an idea in Wes's brain.

He retied the saddle-bag flaps, but left the dynamite on the counter, with the fuse wire laid neatly alongside each bundle.

Midnight still seemed a long way off.

★　★　★

Jack Jimson had only allowed himself one drink. He needed to keep his wits about him. He poured a cup of lukewarm coffee and gulped it down in one go.

He stood by the door and looked out on Main Street.

The sun was setting, in another hour or so it would be dark. Didn't seem likely now that the posse would be back tonight. What the hell were they doing?

Jimson decided to do the rounds, clear his head in the cooler air. He picked up his Remington from the desk and holstered it, grabbed his Stetson and left the office. There was no need to lock up.

As he stepped outside the cooler air was refreshing. A slight breeze brushed his face.

He stepped down from the board-walk and crossed the street. He checked the doors of various stores, said howdy to the few townsfolk about and made his way towards the Golden Horn.

It was the only building in the whole of Main Street that had lights showing. The town council had been planning streetlamps for a long time now, but, as usual, nothing had happened yet.

Jimson walked to the end of Main

before crossing over and checking doors and windows on his way back.

He stopped opposite the Golden Horn. Should he go in?

His mind was made up for him as a horse drew up outside the sheriff's office.

Jimson couldn't see a rider.

Shit! he thought. *Not again!*

Even before he reached the saddled animal, he knew it was the sheriff's horse.

He approached from the rear and immediately noticed the blood and gore that was splattered over the horse's rump.

Patting the sweat and foam-flecked neck of the animal, he saw a boot, trapped in the left stirrup.

A sudden horror filled Jimson's brain. *Jeez!* The word formed in his head but never left his mouth.

He grabbed the boot, it was heavier than he expected.

Then he saw why.

He dropped it instantly and shrieked

like a banshee. The noise echoed down Main Street and pretty soon two or three men appeared on the street. Curtains were pulled back slightly as folks inside wondered what the hell was going on.

Inside the boot was the remains of a leg!

11

Enright joined the group.

Jimson had calmed down by now and, as he looked at Enright, he was sure the man was smiling knowingly.

Surrounded by four of his gunnies, Enright drew on his cigar and blew out a cloud of blue smoke.

'Seems like we need a new sheriff,' was Enright's only comment.

'As the only sworn-in deputy,' Jimson said, 'I'm acting sheriff.'

'Well, for the moment,' Enright said, 'till we have ourselves an election. I'm sure we can come up with a better candidate, eh, boys?'

His men grinned, and Jimson knew what that meant.

'It's too late for a search party tonight,' Jimson went on, ignoring Enright's jibe, 'but come first light I'll need some men. Meet me at the livery at six.'

'What ya gonna do with the leg, Deputy?' one the men asked.

'I'll get a sack. Someone feed and water this animal.'

Jimson entered the sheriff's office, made straight for the bottle and took a big gulp.

Calmer now, he found a sack and went back outside.

Enright and his cronies were walking back to the saloon: he could hear their laughter.

Gingerly, he lifted the boot by the heel and placed it in the sack.

Glad that it was out of sight, he re-entered the office. Much as he had no time for Sheriff West, he wouldn't wish *that* sort of death on anyone.

The door creaked open and in walked Samuel McIntyre, Springfield's ineffectual mayor.

A small, dapper man with Scottish connections, he sported bright red hair and moustache to match.

He was affable enough, but had clearly been voted mayor by the town council because no one else wanted the job, and this man was controllable.

He ran the Saddle Shop, and if it had anything to do with horses, he sold it.

'I just heard the news, Jack. Are we sure it's the sheriff?'

'Well, I ain't too familiar with the sheriff's legs, but it sure as hell is his horse.'

'What happened?' Samuel asked.

'Far as I can figure, somehow, Clint was dragged behind his horse. His boot and part of his leg is all that remains. As to what or who caused it, I have no idea. Eight men rode out of here earlier, so that means there's seven still out there somewhere,' Jimson said.

'And no news on the Parrys?' Samuel asked.

'Not a thing.'

'This sure is a strange business, Deputy, or should I say Sheriff?'

'You can make me acting sheriff,' Jimson said.

'So be it. I'll inform the town council at our next meeting. You've organized a posse, I presume?'

'Meeting at six in the morning, it'll be too dark to go out now.'

'Yes, yes, of course. Well, I'll leave you to it, Sheriff.'

Samuel took his leave.

'Yeah, kinda figured you would,' Jimson muttered under his breath.

★ ★ ★

Dale led Carl straight to Doc Wheelan's place. He had to bang on the door pretty hard, the old doc was as deaf as a post.

The door slowly opened and Doc Wheelan saw Carl. He opened the door wider.

'What the hell, Carl, you know what time it is?'

Dale cut in. 'He's been shoulder shot, Doc, just a crease, but it might have taken a chunk out of his collarbone.'

'And you are?' Wheelan demanded.

'Deputy Smith, we're all that's left of the posse.'

177

Wheelan ushered them in. 'Sit there, Carl. Let's take a look at the damage.'

Cofa, meanwhile, had gone straight to the sheriff's office and sought out Jimson.

'Cofa? I thought you were out with the posse?'

'I was. There's only three of us made it back. Dale and Carl are over to Doc Wheelan.'

Carl went on to tell the tale.

'We had a visit from Ben Ramirez and Nat Baker. Dale saw them off, but they bushwhacked the sheriff an' his men. They're out on the short cut trail near the Dewsburg end.'

'The sheriff's horse made it back here,' Jimson informed him. 'That, and his right leg!'

'Jeez!' was all Cofa could muster.

'What happened to Baker and Ramirez?' Jimson asked.

'Well, when we found Klugg's body, they wanted to know if we'd found anything.'

'Found anything?' Jimson said.

'Yeah, they wouldn't say what, but they were real mean and Ramirez went for his gun. Dale outdrew him and sent them packing. Then we heard the shots. We chased 'em down, the terrain was rough and visibility weren't too good, but I think Dale winged one of them.'

'So Enright's involved,' Jimson said solemnly.

'Sure looks like it, don't know in what way though,' Carl said.

'Get yourself some grub, Carl. Then if you can man the office for a while, I'll go round up some men. We might have trouble coming.'

Carl didn't argue.

Jimson headed straight to Doc Wheelan's place. *This Dale fella seems to be a useful ally*, he thought.

★ ★ ★

Nat Baker could see the few lights that designated Springfield.

He reined in.

'What are we stopping for?' Ramirez grumbled.

'Need to be careful here, Ben. In case those three made it back.'

'What if they did? Enright will take care of 'em. Get me to the doc's. Soon as I'm patched up I'll be fightin' fit.'

'Yeah, right,' Baker said. 'This is what we'll do an' I ain't takin' no truck from you.

'We'll skirt town and ride in from the south side. Get to the Golden Horn and tell the boss what's gone down. He can get Doc Wheelan out to see to you, and we'll be in town with no one knowing.'

Grudgingly, Ramirez agreed.

They rode on and encountered no one as they skirted town. Keeping to the alleyways, they entered Springfield undetected and made it to the rear of the saloon.

Baker dismounted and thumped on the back door. Ramirez was still mounted, blood loss and the ride back had weakened him more than he'd admit.

One of the boys opened the door, his Colt already out. 'Gimme a hand with Ramirez,' Baker said, 'he's hurt pretty bad.'

After holstering his six-gun, the 'slinger helped the wounded man down from the saddle and into the saloon.

'Enright around?' Baker asked.

'Sure, the boss is in his office.'

'Muster a couple of the boys to go with you to fetch Doc Wheelan. Tell him it's a gunshot wound. Drag him here if necessary.'

'Sure thing, Nat.' The man went into the saloon and after a few whispered words, they left through the batwings.

Jimson had reached Wheelan's place a few minutes earlier.

'Had my doubts about you, Mr Smith,' Jimson said without preamble. 'But I guess I was wrong.'

'You sure was,' Carl piped up. 'This man's a hero.'

'Carl, I ain't no hero,' Dale said.

'Cofa told me what went on,' Jimson said. 'You know it ain't over.'

'Any sign of Baker and Ramirez?' Dale asked.

'Not yet, but there will be, you can count on it.' Jimson sighed.

'How many men can you muster, Deputy?' Dale asked.

'Sheriff, now,' Jimson said. 'For what it's worth.'

'If Enright thinks we've got what he's after, he'll come out shootin', or at least his gunnies will,' Carl said.

'I think I know what he's after,' Dale said.

'What?' Jimson asked.

'The key to the safe.'

'I knew it!' Jimson said. 'Enright, Klugg and West were into something, I just can't prove it. It's got something to do with the land-grabbing, I'm certain of that.'

Their discussion was cut short as the front door was nearly knocked off its hinges.

'Doc!' a voice called. 'Open up!'

'Hell, I can guess who that might be,' Dale said.

'Doc! Mr Enright wants you, pronto. You don't open up I'm bustin' this door down,' the voice yelled.

'Better answer it, Doc,' Jimson said. 'Don't let 'em in here. I'll leave by the back door and see what men I can get together. OK?'

Dale and the doc nodded in agreement.

Doc Wheelan went towards the front door.

'All right, all right, hold your horses, I'm comin',' the doc called out. He grabbed his bag and went to the front door.

'Got a gunshot wound, Doc. Let's git goin'. Mr Enright said to hurry.'

Dale heard the front door slam shut, and he breathed a sigh of relief.

He helped Carl on with his shirt. 'You feelin' OK now, Carl?' he asked.

'Much better. What's the plan?'

'Reckon you can get to the sheriff's office?' Dale asked. 'They need all the help they can get.'

'Sure, no problem.'

'Then you head there and back up Cofa.'

Carl grabbed his Winchester, and stood up. His legs were a little wobbly, but he hid it well as he made his way out.

★ ★ ★

Dale was on the horns of a dilemma.

His partners were, he presumed, down at the bank waiting for his return, with or without the key to the safe.

The last twenty-four hours had changed him. He was respected, revered even, and he liked it.

He knew, deep down, he wanted no part of the robbery now. He could make a life in this town.

But should he try and halt the robbery?

He knew he could not betray his partners. But just who was he helping?

He couldn't stand by and watch

Enright take over the town, it would be the death of Springfield.

Dale made his mind up on where his future lay.

★   ★   ★

It was 11.15.

Wes was becoming more and more concerned about Clay. The man seemed to be losing it. He'd caught him talking to the dynamite earlier.

How he wished Dale would return.

The Parrys were asleep, Lucy's head rested on her chest, Luther's was leaning back against the chair.

What to do about them?

He walked to the front door of the bank and held his ear to the blinds, listening. All was quiet. No one had been near the bank all day. He risked a quick look out onto Main Street. It was deserted.

Strange, he thought. The Golden Horn was closed.

Although this was only his third night

in Springfield, he'd noticed the saloon was open way into the wee small hours; poker mostly as the rannies came into town to lose their wages.

Maybe they'd lost it already.

He walked back to the office.

'Dynamite's all ready,' Clay said. He had a strange, manic look in his eye that disturbed Wes.

'Got the rope ready too; all we gotta do is tie the sticks to the safe and *whoosh*! Rich for ever.'

Clay grinned. Wes just stared at him.

'You sure you can handle that dynamite?' Wes asked.

'Sure, sure I can. All I gotta do is insert the fuse wire, light 'em up, and *Boom*!' The manic grin again.

★ ★ ★

Dale reached the sheriff's office at the same time as Jack Jimson.

Jimson had managed to raise four men. Dale looked at them: middle-aged men wearing pistols that had probably never been fired, and carrying rifles.

At least the long-guns were modern, breech-loading Winchesters.

'Looks like we got ourselves seven and a half men,' Dale quipped.

'Hey, who you calling half a man?' Carl said.

'No offence, Carl, but with that shoulder, you can't handle a rifle. We'll need you as back-up. I think Enright's men will try to get in here. If they think we've got the key to the safe they'll stop at nothing to get it.'

Dale looked at each man in turn.

'There's going to be gunplay,' Dale warned. 'We don't know the strength of Enright's men, but I suspect his gunnies are killers. Correct, Sheriff?'

Jimson nodded. 'Sheriff West smoothed over their so-called misdemeanours. We, that is Deputy Smith an' me, reckon something big is going down. We don't know what yet, but it seems clear that Klugg and Enright are — were — in cahoots and that West was involved too.'

'I want two men covering the rear,' Dale said. 'Carl, you and Cofa take care of the rear.'

Dale paused.

'Sorry, Sheriff, I didn't mean — '

'It's OK, Dale. You seem to know what you're doin',' Jimson replied. 'But we need to get the outside covered, too. Maybe someone on the roof opposite?'

'Good thinking,' Dale said. 'You know your men best, but I think you should be in here, Sheriff.'

'I already figured that, Dale. It'll be me Enright will want to talk to.'

Dale nodded in agreement.

'OK, make sure you got plenty of ammo,' Jimson said, opening the gun cupboard, revealing four Winchester rifles, and ammunition stacked neatly in boxes. 'We only got .45s, so change guns if that ain't your calibre.'

Cofa was happy with his twelve-bore, double-barrelled shotgun. 'They try anything back there and they get both barrels,' he said; a slight smile played on the old man's lips.

The men helped themselves to ammunition and one man took out a Winchester lever-action rifle.

'Let's do this,' Jimson said and the men split up to take position.

'Noticed you got a crowbar in there, think I'll take me a wander round the back of the saloon,' Dale said, and winked.

⋆　⋆　⋆

Wilbur Enright was giving instructions to his men. There were ten of them, including the injured Ramirez, who insisted on being in on the action.

Enright split the group into two: one to take station at the rear of the sheriff's office; the other, which he would lead, would approach the front.

'I want no shooting until I say,' Enright said. 'I want to make sure they have the keys for the bank in their possession.'

Ramirez grunted. He wasn't interested in anything but getting even with Dale.

Although his right arm was bound tightly and secured by a sling to his chest by Doc Wheelan, who had been ushered out without ceremony, Ramirez knew he could use his left hand in a cross draw with almost equal effectiveness.

But he wasn't planning on a fair fight. Ramirez was a backshooter at his best, a torturer at his worst.

He was a killer and wasn't fussy on how he went about it.

Enright finished his glass of imported whisky and lit a fresh cigar as he addressed his men.

'If I don't get anywhere with the parley,' he began, 'there's a thousand dollars to the man who brings me the bank keys.'

He paused while the murmur of approval went up. Men began to check their weapons, adding a final bullet to the chambers of their six-guns, then cocking their rifles to make sure a slug was in the chamber.

'OK, you five men skirt the sheriff's

office to the rear and await my signal,' Enright said.

'What signal is that?' one of the men asked.

'A single shot,' Enright answered. 'When you hear that, try to break down the back door and start shootin'. I want no prisoners. Got that?'

The men nodded and silently made their way out of the saloon.

Enright gave them five minutes' start before leading his men through the batwings and down Main Street.

It was exactly 11.30.

12

Dale watched from the deep shadows as five men left the rear of the saloon. He wouldn't need the crowbar to get in as the door was left slightly open, but he kept it handy just in case.

He grinned at their stupidity.

He crossed the dark alleyway and entered the saloon.

It was even darker inside the small corridor he found himself in. He could make out three doors. One straight ahead, and the other two on either side.

He headed for the door ahead. Putting his ear to it, he heard muffled voices, then silence.

So, he thought, they've left.

Slowly and carefully he eased the door open. The saloon was empty, the only light coming from a single oil lamp set on the bartop. Just enough light to see his way to the stairs.

Dale knew where Enright's office was. He climbed the staircase without making a noise. At every step he expected a groaning creak to shatter the silence.

On reaching the upper landing, he paused, listening for any sounds coming from the fallen doves' rooms. But again his ears were stunned by the utter silence.

He reached the door to Enright's office and turned the handle.

It was locked.

Glad now that he hadn't discarded the crowbar, he eased it between the door and frame and gently pulled back. The door snapped open easily and Dale tensed, expecting someone to have heard the noise.

Satisfied that no one had, he entered the office and closed the door silently behind him.

Enough blue moonlight filtered through the large window for Dale to make out the layout of the office. A huge desk monopolized the room. Enright sure had a high opinion of himself, Dale thought as he crossed the room.

He opened each desk drawer in turn, not sure what he was looking for, but knew he would know when he found it.

But he came up with nothing; only one drawer left — and it was locked.

The drawer was no match for the crowbar though. Sliding the drawer open, Dale was filled with hope. Maybe there was something in here?

Riffling through the papers, his eye was caught by a map. Opening it up, he saw it was a map of the area, showing cattle ranches and homesteaders' land. Winding through the map, Dale could just make out in the dim light, a red line marked 'proposed railroad'. So that was it! A railroad was coming to Springfield, and Klugg and Enright had somehow got advance knowledge; so *that's* why the homesteaders had been run off.

Dale folded the map and put it in his back pocket. Now he had some proof for the wrongdoings. From that he deduced that the title deeds to the properties must be in the safe. Now, with Klugg dead, Enright was the sole owner — as long as he had the deeds!

He was about the shut the drawer when he noticed a small, well-used black book in the far corner, almost hidden.

Dale couldn't believe his luck!

Enright was a very thorough, methodical man, and this black book proved it.

Inside he found names and columns of figures. West's name was prominent as the recipient of monies paid 'for services rendered'.

Dale left the saloon building as quickly as he could. He now had the motive for Enright's involvement, and why he had had the sheriff and three of his posse members killed.

He had to get to Jimson.

* * *

'Better get the Parrys out of the office,' Wes said.

'Where will I put 'em?' Clay asked.

'On the far side of the bank, well away from the safe, of course. Where the hell do you think?' Wes said in an exasperated tone.

'No need to bite my head off,' Clay said sulkily.

With a sullen expression on his face he walked over to Luther Parry. Tilting the man's chair on to the two back legs, he dragged him across the office and into the teller's position, where he left him facing the far wall. He then did the same thing with Lucy Parry.

'Done,' he said to Wes. 'We gonna blow that damn thing now?'

'Get the dynamite,' Wes instructed. 'Let's get it tied to the safe ready.' He took out his pocket watch. 'We've still got five minutes to go, I ain't given up on Dale yet awhiles.'

'Let's just do it,' Clay said. 'I'm sick o' this waitin' around. If Dale was gonna come back, he'd be here by now.'

'I said midnight, and *midnight* it'll be,' Wes insisted.

Impatiently, Clay stormed from the office, to return with the two bundles of dynamite and fuse wire. He proceeded to tie them to the safe. One he placed near the keyhole at the top of the safe, the other by the combination dial. 'Don't fuse 'em up till I say so,' Wes ordered.

Clay just looked upwards and muttered under his breath.

★   ★   ★

Again, Dale kept to the shadows as he made his way back to the sheriff's office. He had to cross Main, but he saw that Enright and his men, now halfway to the office, had their backs to him, so he darted across to the alleyway by the general store, where Martha Doyle stood in the window, a vacant expression on her tear-stained face.

She opened up the door as she saw Dale and asked, 'How? How did it really happen? He was a good man. I begged him not to go.' She broke down and sobbed.

The sound of her voice and the convulsive sobs carried on the night air.

Dale wanted to hold the woman and tell her her husband died a hero.

But he hadn't. He'd been swept away by the river's current.

The noise also attracted Ramirez. He turned and, even in the dull light, recognized the man standing outside the general store.

He tapped Baker's arm and pointed. 'I'm going to get him,' he growled.

Keeping his eyes firmly fixed on the figure of his hatred, Ramirez started to walk towards Dale.

In his turn Dale, out of the corner of his eye, saw the approaching figure, noted the bandaged arm and knew straight away who it was.

'Mrs Doyle, get back inside the store, I fear there's gonna be some shootin'.'

Her sobbing halted briefly as she

followed Dale's gaze down Main Street.

'I promise I'll return and tell you everything that's happened, and that includes Jake's unfortunate death. Please, go inside now,' Dale said in a soft voice. Then a sudden thought hit him. 'Here,' he stopped the woman, 'stash these somewhere safe. They're important, an' if I happen to lose out on this gunplay, get them to the sheriff as soon as you can. OK?'

She nodded mutely as Dale handed her the black book and map. She didn't even look at them, but went back into the general store. Dale heard the bolts being shucked. He hoped she went behind the counter out of harm's way.

Dale checked his Colt; six bullet casings showed: he flicked the chamber shut and stepped off the boardwalk.

After the heavy rain Main Street had dried out. The ground was rock hard and rutted. Easy for a man to lose his footing if he wasn't careful.

Dale walked very carefully.

* ★ ★

Enright and his men reached the sheriff's office and fanned out across the street. He looked to his left and right, making sure the men had their weapons out and cocked; he wanted to let Jimson know he meant business.

'Jimson!' Enright called. 'We need to talk.'

Jimson didn't reply straight away. He checked on the two men at the rear of the office, and nodded at Cofa, who nodded back, smiling as he made certain his double-barrelled shotgun was primed and ready for action.

Satisfied they were ready, Jimson called out, 'Talk away, Enright.'

'You know what I want, Jimson, just hand it over and there'll be no bloodshed,' Enright replied.

'Why don't you tell me what it is you want?' Jimson said.

'Don't play games with me, *Sheriff*, you know damn well what I want!'

'*Mister* Enright,' Jimson replied, not

missing Enright's emphasis and returning it in kind, 'I ain't got a clue what you want.'

'The key, Jimson, give me the damn key to the safe!' Enright was losing patience.

'Well, well, now why should I do that? I ain't saying I got it, an' I ain't sayin' I don't, but what makes you think I'd hand it over to a saloon keeper? Only ones entitled to that privilege, as far as I can make out, would be bankers, and they seem mighty thin on the ground right now.'

'I'm warnin' you, Jimson — '

'I got men coverin' you and that scum you employ, Enright, so don't go *warnin'* anyone!' Jimson's voice had an edge to it that chafed Enright.

But his men looked around uncertainly, they had figured this to be a turkey shoot, not a full-blown gun battle.

Warily, the group started to take a few steps back, looking for cover in case the shooting started.

'Cat got your tongue, Enright?' Jimson jibed.

'Let's be reasonable here, Jack,' Enright said placatingly. 'There's a lot of money involved here, I could make you a rich man, a very rich man.'

'Take your men and skedaddle back to that rat's nest you call a saloon afore someone gets hisself killed,' Jimson replied, and waited for Enright's response.

Inside, Enright was seething. Who the hell did Jimson think he was talking to? No one spoke to him like that — and lived!

Enright took out his revolver and was about to shoot when, from further down the street, a shot rang out.

⋆ ⋆ ⋆

Dale stopped. Stood his ground, his feet placed firmly as Ramirez approached. He wasn't a gunslinger, in fact had never had a gunfight, but instinctively, he let his right hand

202

hover an inch or so from the butt of his Colt.

He could see that Ramirez was wearing a cross-draw outfit. *Was he that good?* Dale wondered, but banished the thought instantly.

Doubt never kept a man alive.

Dale could see Ramirez flexing the fingers of his left hand; the man was edgy, Dale was sure about that.

Ramirez shifted his stance as he heard the raised voices from further down Main.

'Go for your gun, if you dare,' Ramirez snarled.

Dale didn't respond. He stood, slightly crouched, poised to move left, right or down at the slightest indication, if necessary.

The two men faced each other silently, their eyes never leaving each other as they both waited to see a weakness, or a hesitation and take advantage.

In a flash, Ramirez's left arm shot across his chest and grabbed the butt of his pistol.

He was quick.

Dale was quicker.

His slug caught Ramirez high up in the chest, spinning the man round. To Dale it seemed to be in slow motion. He could see both fear and surprise in Ramirez's eyes as he spun round. The fall seemed to take an age.

When he hit dirt a small puff of dust shot into the air.

Then there was no movement.

Dale, his Colt still in his hand, walked slowly towards the crumpled body; he knelt and felt for the jugular, just to make sure.

There was a faint beat. He held his finger there for a few seconds more.

Definitely still alive.

'Damn!' Dale muttered. 'This *hombre*'s tougher than he looks.'

At that exact moment, with Dale off-guard, Ramirez's good left hand shot up and gripped Dale's neck like a vice, forcing Dale onto his side in the dirt, his right arm trapped under his body.

He could feel the power in the man's hand as he struggled to breathe, stars appeared in the corners of Dale's eyes and he knew he was choking.

Using what he thought could well be the last of his strength, Dale brought his left fist down onto Ramirez's chest.

The man's grip loosened enough for Dale to get a breath. He hit the man again and again until Ramirez's arm fell away limply.

Now he was dead.

The town was now eerily quiet, no one came to investigate the shooting. It seemed folks were too afraid.

The silence lasted no more than a few seconds before gunfire erupted further down Main.

The shot had been the signal the men at the rear of the sheriff's office had been waiting for.

The men started to fire at the building, bullets ricocheted, wood started to splinter and the small glass window shattered into a million fragments, showering the two men inside.

Cofa waited. He wanted his shots to count; he might not get the time to reload.

Neither man had returned fire yet, there was nothing to shoot at and they waited for the inevitable lull in the attack as they thought about what to do next.

Cofa almost smiled when the shooting out back stopped.

Enright and his men had been taken by surprise as the shooting started. They scurried back across Main Street, seeking cover wherever they could find it. Enright dived behind a water trough, some dived under the boardwalk as they started shooting.

From inside the sheriff's office, Jimson had told the men to hold their fire and wait.

The gunfire stopped as the gunslingers realized no one was firing at them.

It was a waiting game.

★   ★   ★

Wes and Clay automatically drew their weapons as the sound of gunfire exploded.

'What the hell's goin' on?' Clay shouted.

'Keep your voice down,' Wes said calmly.

'Hell, who's gonna hear me in all that racket?' Clay responded.

Wes ran to the front of the bank and peered outside. He had a limited view of Main, but he thought he saw someone diving for cover.

'Whatever's happening out there, it ain't aimed at us.' He paused as a thought occurred to him. 'In fact, this little diversion is all we need,' he added.

'How so?' Clay asked.

'Seems the town's pretty busy at the moment, all that shootin' sure makes a ruckus.'

Clay twigged. 'So we blow the safe?'

'We sure do,' Wes said.

Clay reholstered his pistol and grabbed the fuse wire. A manic leer spread across his face. At last, he thought, some action!

Kneeling in front of the safe, Clay inserted the fuses the way he'd seen it done, making sure they wouldn't fall out. He stood and looked at Wes.

'OK?' Wes asked,

'Yup.'

'We'll wait for more gunfire and when I nod, you light 'em and we dive for cover, got that?'

'Sure, I ain't stupid,' Clay said. He held a box of vestas in his left hand and a match in his right, ready to strike.

13

Dale got to his feet groggily, breathing heavily, as the gunfire started.

He pulled himself together, slipped a slug into his Colt, and, keeping to the shadows, edged his way down Main Street towards the sheriff's office.

He saw movement on the opposite side of the street. The dull gleam as a rifle barrel highlighted by the pale blue light of the moon was raised, taking careful aim at the sheriff's office.

Gripping his Colt in both hands, Dale knelt and also took careful aim.

He held his breath as he squeezed the trigger. He knew it was, at this distance, literally hit or miss.

He was lucky. The rifle barrel shot upwards and to one side. He'd hit his target.

Dale saw the flash of the muzzle as

the man holding the rifle had involuntarily squeezed the trigger.

What he didn't see was where the bullet hit.

Smashing through the bank's front window, the bullet hit Luther Parry plumb dead centre of his back.

He died immediately.

Lucy Parry gave a muted scream as blood showered over her face and dress.

Both Wes and Clay dived for cover, but there were no more shots.

'They got us sussed, Wes?' Clay whispered.

'I don't know. Keep down and keep quiet,' Wes grated.

'Let's get that safe blown and high-tail it outa here,' Clay pleaded.

'Ain't no point if the bank's surrounded, Clay, we'll never make it.'

More shots broke out, but they weren't aimed at the bank.

'What the hell's going on out there?' Wes was confused. 'Something else is goin' on in this town, an' it don't concern us, I reckon,' he added.

He glanced across at the Parrys. Luther's back was covered in blood, he was slumped forward. Lucy had fainted. She, too, was covered in blood and Wes wasn't sure whether it was hers or her husband's!

Wes stood up. 'Reckon that was a wild shot, Clay. Lucky for us, but it sure done Luther Parry no favours.'

'What'll we do now, Wes?' Clay asked.

'We wait and see, Clay. We wait and see.'

★　★　★

Enright was beside himself with rage now. He could see his expected empire crumbling before his very eyes. If the deeds to the land he and Klugg owned weren't in his possession, the fraud would be uncovered and the title deeds to all the land would revert to the bank.

Enright couldn't allow that to happen. 'OK, Jimson. Enough is enough:

we're comin' in! You hear that, Baker?'

'Got ya, boss, we're goin' in!' Baker yelled from the back of the sheriff's office.

Guns exploded once more. Both back and front of the office was a mass of splintering wood and glass. The men inside kept low as they waited for the onslaught.

Dale took the opportunity to dart across Main. He was now on the same side as Enright's men. He made his way to the man he'd just shot and retrieved his rifle. He figured he had a better chance with that than with his handgun.

He waited until Enright's men began to advance across the street, then he fired. He saw a man fall in the dirt, flung forward, face down.

Enright knew straight away that the shot *hadn't* come from inside the sheriff's office.

Enright looked to his right.

In the brilliant flash that lit up almost the entire length of Main Street, he saw Dale.

Then it seemed that all the air in his lungs was sucked out of him and he flew backwards.

* * *

Clay had retrieved the box of vestas and he ran over to the safe. He wasn't about to wait any longer. He struck a match, lit both fuses and ran out of the office.

'You better get down, Wes, there's gonna be a big bang!'

'I told you to wait!' Wes yelled.

'Ain't waitin' no more,' Clay said and ducked down behind the teller's counter.

The explosion was not just ear-splitting, it was ear-shattering. Separated by a few seconds, the first explosion moved the safe back through the rear wall of the bank, leaving the door hanging by one hinge. The second explosion blew the contents sky high, taking the roof off the bank. Main Street was raining paper money.

The rear wall of the bank buckled as

the shock wave hit it, throwing the already dead Luther Parry through the side wall, followed by his wife.

Flames engulfed the dry timber of the tellers' counter, pushing it almost to the front of the bank as the rest of the roof caved in in a shower of sparks and flame.

Clay was crushed beneath the debris and the blast through the manager's thin office walls blew Wes clear across the room.

The whole bank was now a blazing inferno as paper money still fell from the sky, some of it aflame.

Out on Main Street, Enright lay beneath a sheet of corrugated iron, his head all but severed from his body.

Ironically, some of the papers that fell on him were the remains of title deeds.

Windows were shattered on the opposite side of Main, and small fires erupted.

The fight for the sheriff's office halted abruptly. The men out front, those who weren't killed or unconscious, could see what had happened; the men at the rear had no idea what had gone on.

Jimson flung the front door open and, with Winchester raised, rushed out. What he saw took his breath away.

Where the bank had once stood was a sheet of flame and smoke, obscuring the moon. Then he heard shots.

He fell to the ground.

Lifting his head slightly to see if he could find the source of the bullets, he saw spears of flame shoot into the sky.

The gunfire was caused by the fire igniting bullets in guns or belts of whoever was inside.

Dale stood in utter disbelief.

'Goddamn,' he muttered under his breath. 'They used all the dynamite.'

The deafening blast had brought some townsfolk out and they quickly started to form a bucket chain from the troughs on Main, but it was futile trying to douse the flames, the heat was too intense to get anywhere near it.

The people saw the money in the street. Tens, twenties and fifties, the temptation was too great to ignore such a windfall; while men shouted to dampen nearby buildings, others scurried amongst the dirt, grabbing the notes that weren't damaged.

Dale rushed to Jimson to check he was OK, and Carl and Cofa emerged from the sheriff's office, their mouths agape.

From the rear of the bank, there was no sign of the gunnies. The ground shook and buildings trembled as the explosions rent the air and they ran off fearing imminent death.

'What the hell happened?' were the first words Jimson spoke.

Dale was torn between telling what he knew, thereby admitting, at the very least, complicity, at the worst, murder.

He'd made his choice while he was out with the posse, not to be involved in robbery. All he hoped was that Wes and Clay gave up the notion.

Naive perhaps, he now thought, but

nevertheless it had been a fervent hope.

He could see no point now in admitting he was part of the original plan.

Now, he was a part of Springfield.

'Looks like someone was trying to rob the bank,' Dale answered. He helped Jimson to his feet as Carl and Cofa joined them.

'OK,' Dale said, 'let's make sure the whole town doesn't go up in flames.'

Jimson ordered the men on Main to dampen the buildings on either side of the bank, which they managed successfully.

Dale found Enright's body and almost laughed as he saw singed and burned title deeds surrounding him.

'Well, you sure got your hands on those deeds,' he said out loud.

Enright's men had vanished; mercenaries, one and all, they saw no point in hanging around when the money supplier had checked out.

Dale walked around the bank; the flames were dying down now as the tinder-dry timber burned itself out.

Of Wes and Clay, there was no sign, but he did find the Parrys, almost embedded in the wall of the building next to the bank.

Their bodies were charred but recognizable and they were still tied to their respective chairs.

Dale removed his hat, and a tear rolled down his grime-ridden face.

Epilogue

The next day dawned bright and sunny, illuminating Springfield in a yellow light that belied the horrors of the previous night.

The smell of burnt timber filled the air, but that would soon disappear once the site was cleared. The bank was sure to be built again; with the prospect of a railroad coming through they wouldn't waste any time.

News of the railroad spread like wildfire and the citizens of Springfield looked towards a bright and prosperous future.

The evidence that Dale had obtained from Enright's desk was enough to solve one mystery.

The discovery of the Parrys had solved another; still bound and gagged, they were clearly innocent parties held hostage by the failed robbers. So another mystery was solved.

But who the man whose body they had found out on the trail was, and who had killed Klugg, were still mysteries. But not ones the sheriff was too fussed about trying to solve in a hurry. There was too much else to do.

Apart from the clear-up in town, Dale organized and led a group of men with a flat-back wagon, to hit the trail to Dewsburg and pick up the bodies — or what was left of them.

The going was slow, the wagon hindered by the well-rutted trail and the debris that had to be cleared as they hit the short cut. The going was treacherous, but it had to be done.

They came across the first body, still tarp-covered, and loaded it on to the wagon; then they came to Klugg's body.

Signs of the wildlife feasting on his remains turned the men's stomachs, but they rolled him on to a tarp and were about to lift it, when Dale spotted a bunch of keys attached to the dead man's belt.

'Well I'll be a — '

'Goldarn it!' a man voiced. 'Weren't they what all the fuss was about?'

'Ten dead and keys here all the time,' Dale said. 'A final irony.'

It was a further six hours before they found the deputies and another two before they found the remains of Sheriff West, his badge still pinned to his shredded vest.

Having recovered all the bodies, the only missing man being Will Doyle, whose body was never recovered, they continued along the short cut till it met up again with the main trail.

Turning the wagon south, the men headed back towards Springfield.

Dale halted at the junction. He couldn't go back, much as he wanted to, his conscience wouldn't allow it.

'I won't be going back with you, boys,' Dale said.

'What?' a man's voice queried. 'But we need men like you, Dale.'

'My job's finished here and I get kinda itchy feet, if you know what I mean. So I'll be moving on and see what the world dumps on me next time.'

'Hell, you'll be missed, you done a good job with the posse an' all,' the same man replied.

'You all got yourselves a good man in the sheriff's office, an' now that Enright and Klugg ain't around, the town can prosper as a whole and not fall prey to the greed of two men.'

The men reluctantly bade Dale farewill and sounds of 'good luck' and 'thanks' rang in his ears as he headed north.

He never looked back.

★ ★ ★

Back in Springfield, the clean-up was in full swing. The Parrys had been taken to the morgue, awaiting a good Christian burial.

Two bodies were eventually discovered in the ruins of the bank. Both were burned beyond recognition, but it was obvious to Jimson: they were the robbers.

Later in the day Ma Dooley paid a visit on Jimson, to tell him two of her boarders hadn't been back all night and she was worried they might have been injured in the shooting.

Jimson thanked her, and immediately went to the stables where, as he suspected, their animals were still stabled.

'Wes Brown and Clay Leghorn,' Jimson said to himself. 'I'll be danged.'

THE END

We do hope that you have enjoyed reading this large print book.

Did you know that all of our titles are available for purchase?

We publish a wide range of high quality large print books including:
Romances, Mysteries, Classics
General Fiction
Non Fiction and Westerns

Special interest titles available in large print are:
The Little Oxford Dictionary
Music Book, Song Book
Hymn Book, Service Book

Also available from us courtesy of Oxford University Press:
Young Readers' Dictionary
(large print edition)
Young Readers' Thesaurus
(large print edition)

For further information or a free brochure, please contact us at:
Ulverscroft Large Print Books Ltd.,
The Green, Bradgate Road, Anstey,
Leicester, LE7 7FU, England.
Tel: (00 44) **0116 236 4325**
Fax: (00 44) **0116 234 0205**